Praise for Ror Wolf

"Ror Wolf's miniature stories about everyday catastrophes undermine traditional storytelling. They are extremely fresh and incredibly funny."
—Martin Halter, *Tagesanzeiger*

"Wolf takes familiar scraps from crime, romance, and adventure stories, rearranges them and glues them together with a melodious language that drives everything to the extreme. The result is purely absurd and at the same time magical."
—Peter Zemla, *Buchjournal*

"One of the most important contemporary German writers."
—Brigitte Kronauer, Büchner Award recipient

"Ror Wolf has rejected every typical form of storytelling. What is the reader left with? A particular lightness in one's head, a bright glimpse into the madness of daily life."
—*Deutschlandradio Kultur*

TWO
OR
THREE
YEARS
LATER:

ROR
WOLF

Translated from
the German by
Jennifer Marquart

FORTY-NINE
DIGRESSIONS

OPEN LETTER
LITERARY TRANSLATIONS FROM THE UNIVERSITY OF ROCHESTER

Copyright © 2007 by Schöffling & Co. Verlagsbuchhandlung GmbH,
Frankfurt am Main
Translation copyright © 2012 by Jennifer Marquart
Originally published in German as
Zwei oder drei Jahre später. Neunundvierzig Ausschweifungen

First edition, 2013
All rights reserved

Library of Congress Cataloging-in-Publication Data: Available upon request.
ISBN-13: 978-1-934824-70-2 / ISBN-10: 1-934824-70-4

This project is supported in part by an award from
the National Endowment for the Arts.

ART WORKS.
arts.gov

Printed on acid-free paper in the United States of America.

Text set in Minion, a serif typeface designed by Robert Slimbach in 1990 and
inspired by late Renaissance-era type.

Design by N. J. Furl

Open Letter is the University of Rochester's nonprofit, literary translation press:
Lattimore Hall 411, Box 270082, Rochester, NY 14627

www.openletterbooks.org

Contents

TWO
OR
THREE
YEARS
LATER:
*FORTY-NINE
DIGRESSIONS*

In the Mountains

An unknown violinist—a man whose name I wouldn't be able to recall even if I tried—said he'd forgotten, or rather lost his violin, a fact he realized upon being asked to play in a tavern in Gletsch. He thought he might have lost it in Lax on his way through the mountains, where a thick layer of snow had covered the ground. Because of the snow he might not have noticed his violin fall out; it could've fallen out silently, he wouldn't have heard it fall. When he stopped at a tavern that evening and was encouraged to play a little, he discovered in that moment that he no longer had a violin. And so he forever remained an unknown violinist.

Neither in Schleiz,
nor Anywhere Else in the World

A man who prefers anonymity, a certain X—his name is irrelevant—arrives one day, one morning, one afternoon . . . It's all the same in a city whose name we won't disclose. He does nothing, which is what we wanted to report, since what he does do is so insignificant that that's the only significant thing to say about it. He doesn't wear a dark hat, has no umbrella or suitcase. He doesn't have a formal suit or winter coat. His voice cannot be heard. He asks nothing and answers nothing. The only sound he makes is a short, choked cry. His head and face aren't entirely hairy, but they're not entirely bare, either. He walks with such infuriating slowness that you can hardly call this movement walking, so we won't. If he contemplates something it is without feeling; if he touches something it is without reason. I think he is a man without purpose. More often than not he sits curled up, wrapping himself in his arms with his head buried between his knees, and sleeps—or appears to be sleeping. From time to time he breaks his silence with a shout that is utterly meaningless and expresses neither sentiment, nor need. He doesn't know fear, but he also lacks courage; he doesn't seem to have any friends, but also seems impervious to sadness. I was never able to sense any feeling of contentment in him. Sometimes, when called by name, he'll turn his head. Usually he doesn't look around, but instead sits in the midst of the world like a stone. But Collunder's assumption—that he lacks any awareness of his surroundings and his immediate situation, that he knows neither love, nor hate, has neither friend, nor foe—is false. And one day I'll prove it.

One Sunday, or Monday, or whenever—on a day—this man shows up at my office, or somewhere else. He shows up without a sound and without any discernable movement, puts one foot in front of the other until he reaches me. Then he lifts his hand; he lifts his hand with astonishing quietness and thoughtfulness, and extends it to me. At this point we'd perhaps expect a word, a remark, a message, and we're right to do so. This meeting, at this extraordinarily slow speed, remains unforgettable: the slow handshake, the unbelievably polite tip of the hat, the way he removed it, and everything else he did. However, it is for entirely personal reasons that I do not relay the following to the public.

Various Ways to Lose Peace of Mind

One day a waiter from Cologne went to an otologist's office. The waiter had stuck a bean in his ear and couldn't get it out. The doctor removed the bean and charged him thirty Deutschmarks, but the waiter only had twenty-five. So the doctor took the bean, stuffed it back in the waiter's ear and showed him the door. Another man, a window dresser from Berlin, was decorating the shop window for a bedding department. Suddenly, he grabbed his chest and collapsed silently onto one of the freshly made beds. He lay there for three days, and no one noticed him. His coworkers thought he was on vacation, while passersby took the dead man for a mannequin. A third man, a salesman from Denver, was driving through Arizona in his black Chrysler—through the beautiful city of Phoenix—when he suddenly heard shouting through the open window. He thought he had run over someone, but didn't find anyone injured on the street. The shouting continued; then the salesman finally realized it was coming from down in the sewer. A police officer showed up and found a road worker who had fallen through a hole in the tunnel system four days earlier. Confused and starving, the worker stood there in the sludge and kept asking for milk and cake. That's not all. A fourth man, an employment counselor from Mönchengladbach, took a vacation to New Caledonia and went on a diving excursion. When he resurfaced after some time, the boat that had brought him to this corner of the world had vanished. Someone had forgotten this man, this employment counselor from Mönchengladbach, in the Pacific Ocean. As he began to grasp his situation he started to shout; he shouted and shouted, but his words were swept away by an oncoming storm.

Laughter

A nice, but somewhat ill-bred man lived in Bitsch. One day he met a woman. Around dusk, as the sun sank behind the mountain, a laugh was suddenly heard. The next morning and that afternoon this laugh was heard again, only a little louder. I will never forget the following night in Bitsch. I heard the laughing, and this nocturnal laugh was of such tremendous strength that I went to the window and looked out. There I saw the ill-bred man. He sat in a corner of the world, his mouth open as wide as it would go. It looked unsafe, but it didn't really mean much. A throaty moan suggested great inner excitement. But it's entirely trivial and hardly worth mentioning. I remember shouting something: *What's so funny?* But I have to admit I could care less about the answer. So for now we'll lose sight of this man from Bitsch and concern ourselves with someone else.

An Approximately Forty-Year-Old Man

An approximately forty-year-old man from Olm was on his way to Ulm on Monday, when an approximately thirty-year-old man approached him and hit him over the head with a bottle. The blow occurred without any apparent reason. The men—one of whom then left for the nearby train station and onto the express train to Elm—did not know each other. In Elm, a resort town located at the foot of the Tschingelberg where slate was once mined, one of these men climbed the Rotstock, crossing over the Panixer Pass and ending near the Alps. It was an easy and rewarding ascent, which his notes—later found next to him under the snow—recorded in detail.

In a French Kitchen.
In a Swiss Lake.
In a Berlin Closet.

The inside of my head no longer works; it has to go, a Frenchman wrote in the margins of a newspaper in France. He then placed three sticks of dynamite on his head, tied down the bundle with a fuse, and attached the end to a kitchen timer. His wife found him two days later, headless and next to the stove. That's not all I want to tell. Angry, a man threw his golf bag, clubs and all, into Lake Geneva; he'd missed the hole three times. Then it occurred to him that his car keys were also in the golf bag. This man, a Swiss from Bern, jumped into the lake and drowned. At the same time, three seventy-year-old men met their deaths while playing cards in a closet. As the closet door suddenly banged shut, one of the men lit a match so they could see their cards. All three men burned. This was in Berlin, near Nollendorfplatz.

The District Office Employee Outing

During a company picnic in Dux, a well-dressed woman suddenly rushed to a man lying on the ground, bent over him, and whispered a few words into his ear, at which point they quickly disappeared into the neighboring darkness. I'll leave it to the reader to decide how this story continues, but I'm sure he'll draw the right conclusion in order to continue on to the next page.

The Current Conditions in Cologne

Shortly before midnight in front of the Cologne train station, a man was approached and asked if he was Indian. He denied that he was, and received a friendly embrace. That was Monday. Tuesday things were different. On Tuesday, it was reported that a male cyclist had been hitting a female cyclist in front of the concert house for a considerable amount of time. Both were members of the City Chamber Orchestra; they shared an apartment and had come to blows over the repair of an instrument. During the fight, the woman bit the man's arm and, in return, he hit her in the glasses so hard that she ended up with a bloody cut by her nose. The cause of the dispute— the instrument—was not mentioned again that day. The following day, Wednesday, a man drove his car into the wall of the chamber of commerce. He had wanted to talk to a woman, but she had outright rejected him. So he said he would drive his car into the chamber of commerce—and he did. This man, a wine salesman, was completely drunk and not in any condition to give a statement regarding his character; what's more, he'd probably lost all sense of composure. A little while later he collapsed and stayed with some acquaintances until Thursday. On Thursday, a man on the second floor of the post office hit a woman over the head with a telephone receiver. Right before that, a carrier for the district court had taken a bottle and hit a janitor over the head with bone-chilling indifference. That same day, on the second floor of the electric company, a custodian hit an electrician with a vacuum cleaner tube. As the electrician fled, the custodian chased after him a few steps, and is said to have laughed loudly. The next day, Friday, a dispute developed in which a welfare recipient punched a welfare employee in the mouth and ear, and then put him in a chokehold. Another man, who thought it would turn into a brawl, tried to intervene, but things had gone too far. Which is why several men bolted out the door and began randomly hitting bystanders. Without knowing the exact course of events, I find the behavior of the above-mentioned men outrageous. But instead of getting involved, I'll content myself with considering it a product of the current situation in Cologne—about which we no longer have to wonder.

At the Barbershop

A man, a sales broker, walked through the door and fired six shots at a naked dentist, painting the bed red. A naked woman jumped out of the bed and disappeared through the back door. The dentist died, and the broker fled the country. But that's not the story I wanted to tell. I wanted to tell the following story: A barber owes his life solely to the quick-wittedness of a dentist who'd just been given a shave. The dentist was able to grab the hatchet that a dissatisfied butcher pulled out from his jacket with the intent to deliver a fatal blow to the barber's head. A detective happened to be passing the barbershop during the commotion, which took place on Saturday, but wasn't reported until Monday. The detective subdued the butcher with an armlock and brought him straight to the station. The butcher, a man from Mol, was unhappy with his haircut and had therefore taken up the hatchet. However, such events are extremely rare, so it's not entirely necessary to go too far into the details.

Arrival at 15:25

An ex-cook, an ex-engineer, and an ex- . . . an ex-caretaker, an ex-fireman and an ex-what . . . a doctor, an ex-doctor, and an ex-interpreter with well-manicured hands, and an ex-teacher, an entire group of ex-teachers, and more and more ex-teachers returning from Africa and America, from Asia and Australia, from the most distant lands in the world, all left the train station in Bonn and blended into the crowd. This happened at the exact time I was sitting in the station café one afternoon, beginning and ending, beginning and ending the account you've just read, during which time I had nothing more than a glass of mineral water—which now, at 15:30, has been emptied to the last drop.

An Instance of Deep Contentment

On Tuesday night, a stranger opened the front door of the Kolb Pub in Worms, stepped up to the bar, ordered a beer and downed it in a single swig, then closed his eyes and gave off an overall impression of deep contentment.

A Misfortune in the West, on May 13th

One evening, a homeless man sat on the rail of the overpass on Mombacher Strasse in Mainz. Another man, who was strolling on the opposite side of the street, saw the homeless man's legs suddenly shoot up and his body pitch backward into the indiscernible deep. On this same evening, a man in Bonn fired a shot into the air, but no one heard it. An hour later in Lindau, a car ricocheted off of a tree with an enormous crash, flipped over and sank silently into the moon's reflection on the lake. Another man, who had just driven by on his way back from Kaufbeuren, reported seeing the bright tail-lights sinking into the water right before he drove into an electrical box and sustained a head injury. Yet another man, a Pole, a roofer, lost his balance in Darmstadt and plummeted from the roof. At the same time a pastry chef was traveling in Cologne; he turned around and at that moment saw a waiter get out of a car and drop his keys into the sewer. The waiter, said the pastry chef, lifted the black man-hole cover and lay on his stomach, but his keys were no longer in reach—the waiter couldn't find a foothold on the smooth, rounded walls, and he slid deeper and deeper into the drain until his head eventually dipped into a dark layer of sludge and water. That was in Cologne. In Koblenz, a man, a salesman, stood by a mailbox for a moment. Nearby stood a woman, a saleswoman, who was ready to cross the street. At that moment, right as the salesman turned around and lightly grazed the woman, a man from Bad Ems, a cyclist, biked toward them. That night an agent, a man from Marl named Sapp, heard a body drop onto the roof of his car as he was driving to Moers; he only stopped when he saw blood dripping down the side window.

The agent called the police and explained that a heavy shadow had fallen onto his car and shattered the windshield. The subsequent investigation revealed that this agent, this man from Marl, was not only under the influence of alcohol, but also that he didn't have a driver's license. He also wasn't an agent, wasn't from Marl, and wasn't actually driving to Moers. He was not the owner of the car and his name was not Sapp—other identification papers issued to different names were found. Also found were a locked handbag, the owner of which was unknown, and a suitcase that could not be opened. Next to the bags lay a pump-action shotgun—loaded, safety off, and, as was later learned, stolen. Around the same time, or a little earlier, a homeless man in Mainz sat on the rail of the Mombacher Strasse overpass and saw stones fall from the sky. He appeared to regard their falling with great interest, and didn't budge until a large stone finally hit him in the head, causing his legs to snap upwards as he pitched back into the indiscernible deep. I found this man while on an evening stroll along Binger Strasse in Mainz. Afterwards, he explained the incident to me and I recorded it.

The Power of Song in Nevada

You have asked me, Sir, for my opinion on the Sound Expansion Plans. There is nothing I can say about them. I admit that I value sound. I've traveled throughout this entire loud, reverberating world. I've traveled out of a profound disposition for the echoing sea. I've heard ship bands and chamber orchestras, I've experienced the howling of the wind and the wild shouts of sailors—but all of that is nothing compared to the men's choir I heard in Nevada. I would, if you would permit me, gladly talk about the awfulness of the men's choir in Nevada, if only I weren't so certain that all remarks regarding its awfulness have already been made. Incidentally, the worst men's choir I heard was not in Nevada, but here in Olm, here in this very room, where you are asking me for my opinion on the Sound Expansion Plans.

Believe me, Sir, I know what I'm talking about. At the start of this story I sat on a sofa among the cushions, and reflected on singing. I saw nothing I hadn't seen before. The sounds I heard, I had *also* heard before. People came into the room. I can't say that their coming in surprised me; in fact, they came in continually, there was no end to it and it bore no relevance to my expectations, but it wasn't memorable.

Perhaps you would like to know who came in, Sir. I can't help you, I don't remember anymore. All I know is this: an hour later I didn't hear any more sounds. At the time I should have said: *I hear nothing*. I couldn't sleep that night, Sir, and I have no idea how many nights I couldn't sleep—three, four, five nights I couldn't sleep, or more, six or seven nights—and I really wanted to, I actually wanted to sleep, but I couldn't, Sir.

The floor, if I may mention it, was covered in glass. I hadn't previously paid attention to the floor, but suddenly I saw glass splinters near the smoking table; I saw a pile of cigar ash and later, Sir, I spotted a few peanut shells on the floor. People passed by, hunched over and mute, with plates and glasses they could not put down.

Suddenly, for some inexplicable reason, I had a cigar in my hand and I think I said a few words. But the people didn't hear me. I saw three men in an alcove making themselves comfortable, smoking from beneath their hats—I'll never forget it. The first spoke. The second objected. Then the third spoke. The first had nothing to object to in return. I'll never forget it. I'll also never forget how the fourth man appeared. He seemed to be freezing to death from the coldness that he himself exuded; he didn't take off his coat, or his hat, and even kept his gloves on. His face was frozen and everything around him in this room froze, cloaked by a thin, icy layer. I saw breaths freeze by the window. The water in the flower vases froze, and through an open door I could see into the kitchen, where an enormous icicle grew from the faucet and bored through the large slab of meat sitting in the sink. I think my lips froze together, and it's possible my teeth froze together behind my lips. I'll never forget it, Sir.

Someone must have then slammed the door. I had a cigar in my hand, and a man was positively appalled when I blew smoke towards him. The cigar, he said, and stamped his thumb into the ashtray, should be considered extremely harmful and should be done away with. He based this, I believe, on the opinion that tobacco is a luxury one could forgo without harm to life or limb. I saw the cigar in my clammy hand, and after the smoke dissipated I made another discovery: a man lying on the floor, motionless. I saw these puddles of beer, these burn marks in the carpet, the trampled butts of cigarettes, and I saw champagne bottles falling over and spilling, women's shoes, paper napkins, bread crumbs, pretzel sticks, pickle slices, and dark, skewered olives.

To make a long story short: I asked this man what that soft, shimmering mass lying on the floor was. He said he didn't know, and asked what I thought of the Sound Expansion Plans. Sir, I said and looked for a while out the window at the wintry mountain peak, I think nothing of the Sound Expansion Plans. I recall he straightened himself up a bit and talked with me. Naturally, the conversation was only about my trip through Alabama which, at the time, had been hit by severe storms.

Suddenly, the door flew open, and there, fat and dark, stood the director of the pump factory. In comparison to this tremendous man the room seemed small, utterly insignificant. The worst was generally to be expected. But the air suddenly whistled out of this man. He shriveled up in a single moment and vanished into an armchair with a sigh. Someone took the opportunity and began to speak. I saw dry biscuits on the floor and moist, rolled-up fish. A man asked what I thought of the Sound Expansion Plans. I think nothing of it, I said. I saw the disarticulated heads of women, more and more women came in; the curtains billowed and suddenly there were no mirrors, no lighting and no washrooms and no coat racks, no cloakroom. Sir, I said, the Sound Expansion Plans don't interest me. I saw a massive crease in the carpet and literal swells; the floor rolled, it bulged and burst open in several places. Where do you want to go, a man asked. I'm leaving, going to Ohio, I answered. What will you do in Ohio. That's what I'd like to explain to you, Sir.

The heat that day was so intense, that I didn't dare lay my bare hands on the piano that stood in the direct sunlight. So my astonishment was even greater when I saw a man lift the cover and begin to play. What an evening. There was conversation, music, everything was there, everything was in full swing; there was also comfort and ease. As I stood up, I saw record sleeves and wrenched-off knobs on the floor.

The smoking table I had passed wasn't really significant—it had absolutely no importance in this context. Someone approached me and offered me his hand casually, as if no vast destiny lay between us. What do you think of the Sound Expansion Plans, he asked. I didn't know what he meant. I want to explain it to you, the man said. I saw complete strangers near the bookcase. I approached them, I drew close to them, but couldn't find a single familiar face. It was an unforgettable moment, Sir. When I looked outside, the woods were already coming into leaf. In the evening I came to a high, all-white wall, and someone began tapping on it—incidentally it was me, and I tapped and tapped with something about the size of a man's middle finger. At the same time I saw opened newspapers blowing across the floor.

Once, near the heater, several women surrounded me. I wasn't bothered by this, I poured something into my glass and was already in a different place. Later I passed the smoking table two, three, four times, and as I reached the table a fifth time, I saw the small sofa I'd been sitting on, I saw the small cushions and sat down.

I then saw a woman—who I'd never seen before—running her fingers through her hair, and when I looked up again after some time she was still preoccupied with her hair, so soft, so sleek. I think she laughed lightly and lifted it, Sir, she lifted her hair and only the drumming of rain on the veranda could be heard. I saw her shiver and then sigh deeply, while a well-dressed man who had been sitting next to her shifted back. He stood up, he withdrew his hand from under her skirt, and left. He simply left the room, while this woman began to light a very long, thin cigarette.

I sat on the sofa, Sir, and bit my cigar, I bit a small piece off the end, the end of this cigar, and at the time nothing unnerved me. I saw fur coats and large hats lying on the floor, and this man on the floor was still talking to me; he spoke of the Sound Expansion Plans that I should take into consideration. I think that at that time I just forced his mouth shut; at some point in the middle of the evening, the one I'm recounting, I forced his mouth shut, then picked up the ashtray—three times in succession, to be exact. The trace, or more precisely, the tracks, led out of this room into the corridor, and then everything vanished into the sea, everything disappeared and so on and so forth. Suddenly the earth began to tremble, the sea rushed up, something swam through the water, and the people nodded.

In the next moment, I realized I was lying on the carpet with my glass in hand. Through the window I saw a house collapse, I saw a man, if I may mention it, a small, blotchy man, and I shouted something in his ear, but he didn't understand me. On the floor I saw opened boxes and peeled-back sardine tins, and suddenly I saw animals falling from above, from the ceiling, and smacking against the floor. I think they were magnificently heavy snakes, though I didn't understand where they came from. Then I saw small, very thin snakes slithering out from under the armchairs and the carpet, or pouring through the window in great numbers. Snakes, Sir, coiled up, completely smooth, with ice-cold eyes, hanging motionless. They seemed to be comfortable and made no sound other than a friendly hissing. I was the epitome of calm during all of this, Sir. A dark lump in the middle of the room caught my attention; I also noticed a rising and falling, a visible breathing—then the lump quickly split apart, and something ten meters long uncurled, spread itself around the entire room with extraordinary speed and draped over the furniture. I watched with particular amazement, without losing my composure.

The wind blew in and billowed the curtains. The sudden storm pushed me back into the cushions. And I heard a sound like someone continuously mopping the floor, an infinite mopping, until this floor was worn completely thin, Sir. It took zero effort to push a finger through it, this floor that had been mopped thin, and it splintered with only the slightest sound, like a string being plucked, Sir, and something swelled up from the bottom, something horribly fleshy, squeezing up—perhaps a song. A terrible, festering, skull-crushing song.

Sir, you asked for my opinion. But I have nothing to say. Maybe now, at the end of this story, I can take my time and say that I feel capable enough to provide more and greater details about the room where I lingered for quite some time. Perhaps I will talk about the location of the room and the state of the furniture, and naturally about the condition of the window, the window and the curtains. After that, if you permit me, I'll treat the room as a whole, as a unified whole. I'll try to give an idea of its contours. The movements that occur in this room stir my imagination: the sounds, the smells. Perhaps I'll talk about them next. How the room is wallpapered, how I'm interested in its colors and the people who inhabit it. Afterwards I'll describe the song, which is essentially indescribable. Though I have nothing more to say than that.

In conclusion, I'll take my leave, Sir, I'll take my leave with these thoughts, or these words. The rain would beat against the window. A gust of wind would blow through the room. An incredibly deep sigh might be heard when the door is opened, then closed again with a slight sound. A man would then go out, and it would be me—the man going out would most likely be me. Later I would go somewhere; I would know where I was going. Of course the landscape would have to be covered in snow, the black smoke stacks would have to be smoking, the moon would have to drift swiftly through the fog, over the slaughterhouse district, the freight shed, the train station grounds. Because in this way my story, which is shorter than I'd feared, and which I titled *The Power of Song in Nevada*, could still be brought to a reasonable ending.

An Incident Last September at the Bad Tölz Station Restaurant

It's true that, until now, there was little discourse concerning Noll. One could also assume that it's difficult to say something about Noll. I have a completely different opinion. I know a lot about Noll. Noll was a difficult, unlucky man, but let's leave Noll—about whom there is nothing to say—out of it, and talk about Mauch. Mauch was a difficult, unlucky man, and believed his situation last September to be worse than it actually was. There may be cases where such feelings are understandable, but not now, not in this story, not with Mauch, and not in September. We find ourselves, by the way, in one of those famous, oft-described moments in literature, in which a woman at the Bad Tölz station restaurant faints at the sight of Mauch. We are involved in a situation that was not only described by Scheizhofer in his report, but also by Lemm and Collunder: Mauch sits on the left side of the table waiting for brunch, another man, hunched over deep in thought with teacup in hand, sat next to him—the famous young pianist Hofmann, whom I've already introduced to my readers as the driver of a car. His flashy performance on the piano is irrelevant here. He sets his teacup down when he sees the woman fall, and glances out the window. I couldn't understand what he said, and I didn't write it down. In the background, which plays an utterly insignificant role in this story, the public-in-transit takes its place at the restaurant tables, in this atmosphere lightly clouded by cigarette smoke. The aforementioned Mauch suddenly turned right—I don't know why, maybe to call out the woman in question for her striking behavior, which is possible—while in front of him, in front of Mauch, a traveling salesman and a train engineer discussed with lively gestures what was on the wall to the right, above the buffet table in this snow-covered station restaurant in Bad Tölz. It was a painting. One that is often described in art history classes. In this painting, a woman sits on a cold—Scheizhofer says: *hard*, Lemm says: *smooth*, I say: *cold*—rock. The gaze of this remarkable, swollen woman is directed downward, her left hand grips the chin of a naked man standing with his arms poised between her legs. It is certainly not a portrayal of pure disaster. It also does not suffice as a portrayal of the conditions in Bad Tölz; however, it says a lot about the idiosyncrasies of overgrowth, the flora in September, the quality of nature in this region beyond the artificiality of the rising moon reflected on the hat of a man standing to the right of the station buffet in September. One can see—and this is what I'd like to describe to my readers—that in this moment, at the station buffet in Bad Tölz, in the haze of numerous lit cigarettes, something is torn open. It's the *Tölzer Zeitung*, it's being snapped open, or perhaps actually being snatched away from a man standing at the buffet who has yet to be mentioned. I don't know his name, by the way. So, this man snaps open the newspaper, the *Tölzer Zeitung*, with a deep sigh, while the heads of the other patrons are almost completely covered in the haze of the lit cigarettes. I won't describe those sitting in the smoke, the conditions of the outside world and the relations in Bad Tölz—Scheizhofer described all of that. As we already know, Scheizhofer speaks solely of conditions; he talks about nothing but conditions and relations. Lemm doesn't make a single mention of these things; he only talks about light and the objects it illuminates in the evenings before the train Mauch wants to take to Murnau departs. In any event, Collunder has stopped reporting. And at the moment nothing else occurs to me that I could describe. Maybe a distant observer with an overnight bag stands next to the swinging door, next to the vending machine, and looks as if he had an extremely meaningful message to communicate to us. Maybe he wants to tell us that the building in which we have stopped is not the Bad Tölz station restaurant at all—but it's already too late for this.

Not a Word

Not a word was uttered by an unknown man as he embraced an unknown twenty-year-old woman from behind on Boppstrasse. She was able to get away and call for help. What the man actually wanted is unknown.

One Day, a Thursday, in December

One day. I'm embarrassed that I have to report to you about a very ordinary, absolutely miserable little event that happened one day. I have not forgotten that day, which I fabricated. Suddenly I heard the door open, which I also invented. One day—yes, just a moment—one day the door opened and that's when it all started. It went like this: I poured hot water into an imaginary teacup and brewed myself a cup of black, Chinese tea. Moments later I made up an old, unmarried man; I wanted to continue on with my reports when this man opened the door with a subdued, Far Eastern smile. He sat in the Chinese armchair and watched me as I wrote. I gave this man a name, but I've forgotten it. I greeted him politely and shook his hand. Good evening, Mr. Wong. He stood up—I just imagined him standing—he stood up slowly, he rose and threw on a small, silk coat: a coat. I imagined a coat, a small, silk, Chinese coat, and described a very gentle, silky throwing-on. That was on a Thursday in December. And as I thought about letting this man walk out the door, he vanished. That was a really terrible beginning, but a very good ending. But I don't want to end quite yet. I'd like to continue. One day I found myself on a train trip through Colorado and, as I glanced out of the sleeper car window in the morning, I saw that we had stopped at a small station. The rain, turbid and nearly black, fell from above, and as we left the train station a terrible storm began, in which everything I imagined was lifted into the air: hats, umbrellas, roofs, the entire area surrounding the train station, all imagined by me. In this moment I tried to laugh my fears away even though the storm's bluster crushed nearly every joke. The train thundered over the long, iron bridge—which I made up—and propelled it deep into the mountains. I glanced at the clock and took note; it was eight o'clock in the morning, on a Thursday, in December. And right at this moment, a shout compelled me to look back. Again, this is the transition into a new story and the opportunity to continue writing—one day. One day. One day an opportunity to continue writing came. I invented a café and a small, freestanding table where I sat and continued to write. I trusted everything: the paper, the pencil, the objects around me, the people quickly passing by. I was the definition of a relatively calm person; time played no role in my life. I sat in the café and contemplated an ordinary little trip. Naturally, back then I constantly thought about ordinary little trips, but all of these thoughts, with one exception, weren't worth mentioning. And it's only because of the people who request from time to time in passing that I report something exceptional about these thoughts that you will hear what they're about. One day. I traveled straight through Ontario by train; I was alone in the compartment and wished I had some company. So I thought up an unknown man, who immediately began to lower the window a bit, just a little, it's been a while since then—I barely remember it being lowered. But suddenly I believed that this man was about to share something remarkable with me; it seemed it was unpleasant information that concerned this train trip through Ontario. The storm was getting stronger. The ground was split open, grated apart by drought. Back then I described the bleakness of the mountains, the entire area crusted over, like a scab; trees and bushes pale as cement, a grey and wind-ravaged place, colorless, sickly, mangy grass, the wind—I wrote at the time—the rattling wind, with its dry cough, or perhaps resounding, rather rustling, a rustling area. Yes, that's it, flattened against the earth by the wind, rustling and scarcely moving, barely moving, almost no movement. This man I spoke of, the man I made up, who had a long, thin beard and who wore a bag-shaped head covering, was not tall and not short, and, by the way, he didn't live long. As it grew dark he stopped moving, fell back into the cushion and did not move again. A while later when I grabbed and shook him, he was already cold and forgotten. However, the favorable circumstances I was in allowed me, at this point, to begin a story that dealt with an imaginary man. I by no means intend to lecture my reader at length; this man, a Chinese apparition I made up, was one of the men you'd meet near the large ports, and was someone who no one really quite knows how they live, but they do. This man, this man I invented, had something predatory about him, something very dangerous. Incidentally, as it would later turn out, it had to do with a man of little significance, but that shouldn't bother us. The most significant thing about him was how slow he moved. The events of this day in December were suitable enough to observe and describe these movements. I have to tell you, I have never before observed and described such slowness. At the end of the third day I heard a scratching. I won't tell you anything about this scratching. Naturally, I could recount numerous other things, but I won't say anything about this scratching. Maybe I'll tell you something about the rain; I'll imagine a torrential rain, a rain that falls thick and black from above. Or I'll talk about snow, snow I make up—I'd imagine a terrible snow storm, I'd imagine a house that slowly disappears in the accumulating snow, or I'd make up a completely different story one day, on a Thursday, in December.

An Almost Complete Portrayal
of the Conditions in Maybe Waabs

A man, whose name I've thankfully forgotten, came up to me and said something that I've thankfully forgotten. It happened in a city whose name escapes me, on a day I don't remember, or on a night I don't remember. I can't say anything about the weather. I also can't say what happened later. I know nothing about the beginning and even less about the end. I did, however, notice that never in my life had I experienced anything quite as dangerous as I had in this moment. But I forgot about it.

The Laughter of the Sailors

I need to tell you a few things about a man you don't know. You have never heard of this man, and after my report you most likely still won't know who he is. You'll never know his name, his origin, or even have an inkling as to what he is thinking, but you will learn something of his life—that I can promise. You see, lately, I've managed to observe his way of life and write it down.

I can claim to be able to describe this man better than anyone else before me, though I am not the first to mention him. You'll find somewhat credible descriptions in the reports by Schall—a naturalist based near Schleiz—whose observations proved to be generally correct. Unfortunately, they were riddled by their own invalid opinions and notions, and were distorted by the statements given by the residents of Schleiz, to which I was unable to attribute much validity. According to Schall, this man led a lonely, nocturnal life, and would therefore be less noticed than the other men in the area.

Schall was the first author to reflect extensively on this man. He said things about him that, even back then, in the spring, would make me shake my head, and still give me cause to doubt today, in the following autumn. For instance, Schall claims this man never left the region around Schleiz. This is an inaccurate statement. I saw the man myself near Celle, and obtained credible bits of information regarding his stay near Vacha, as well as on the other side of the Weser River. To the best of my knowledge, people had also run into him in Berlin, or thereabout, and—according to my own observations—in Vienna. Of course, he rarely resides in the south and

I cannot say with certainty whether or not he sometimes stays in Zurich, as Ramm claims.

In the summer, this man took first place in a wrestling match in Koblenz, where he had unexpectedly turned up. As I saw him walking away that time, nodding his head in his immense superiority, I got my first glimpse of what the art of wrestling was really about. But that's not all. The following day he sent every opponent to the mat with the help of his fists. The women attending this performance supposedly cried out at the phenomenal use of his right, and they continued to shout long after this man disappeared into the haze of the locker room tunnels. That was in Cologne. However, in Schleiz, his hometown, so to speak, he apparently doesn't cause much of a stir.

In Schleiz, this man usually moves about as if he's completely blind; at least it seems so, even when he sits there with his eyes open and darting back and forth, not taking notice of the slightest things in front of him. As night fell, wrote Schall in his reports, I waited for him to finally rise. But he didn't stir; he showed absolutely no sign of stirring, even though I waited until pitch dark for him to move. I didn't even see anything over the course of the night, no motion, not even a stirring. He just sat there, didn't shift; and as day finally broke, he was still sitting motionless in this spot, leading me to believe that he sat without moving once throughout the duration of the night. He behaved similarly throughout the following day, and I became convinced that the conditions in Schleiz made this man entirely incapable of moving, stirring, or getting up off the floor. And as he wouldn't eat anything, I decided to kill him, so that I could incorporate him into my scientific collection. I attempted, wrote Schall, to crush his windpipe, but noticed that I couldn't squeeze my fingers together enough to restrict his breathing. Thus I was compelled—entirely against my feelings, by the way—to hit him several times over the head, and as he received each of these blows he uttered a short, hoarse cry. Until then, and with this single exception, he had been entirely mute, entirely mute, wrote Schall. Every inconvenience left him indifferent, and only when I held up a piece of meat did he open his enormous mouth—apparently in order to frighten me—but he never showed any intent to bite me.

Here I would like to dispute Schall's claim—who I think is a poor observer—since this man, whose name I've unfortunately forgotten, stood up; he simply got up out of his chair without any difficulty. That was in Marl. The man got up with such ease in Marl that it astounded me. He carried out several movements that I'd like to describe as dancing—dancing. I remember a woman twirling by, gliding with him the entire night. I can also recall sounds: clunky pianos, a scratching, a rubbing, a rubbing together of bodies and an occasional groan. As he glided he gently lifted and lowered himself in the air; he floated, performing the most beautiful turns with the greatest of ease in the company of the aforementioned smiling, sleek-ly dressed woman, whom he simply bit into as they danced.

As it happens, his climbing ability was also notable, which is in complete contrast to Schall's claim. In Paris I saw him scale the Eiffel Tower with great speed—smiling, and with a small backpack—then disappear at the top with a wave. At that moment, this man did something profoundly striking. He appeared to be standing on air with his body upright, and by doing so differed so greatly from Schall the naturalist's statements, that I began to doubt all of Schall's other claims. He seemed to shimmer. It was, if I remember correctly, the type of shimmering that is cloaked by a type of fog. In my opinion, he surpassed everything that I had seen thus far.

Schall has doubts about this. His gait, writes Schall, is creeping and deliberate. When it comes down to it, his typical gait is a slow plod; the fastest pace he's capable of is a slightly more rapid lumber.

It is impossible for him to turn around abruptly. Corpulence prevents it. That said, if he wanted to increase his speed to the maximum, he could only do so by going in a straight line, or in a very broad arc, and only during the darkest time of night and in the blackest corner on earth. Light seems to really cause him pain. Because he lacks the ability to quickly survey his surroundings, anything unfamiliar upsets him. To him, the world seems extremely dubious. He is afraid of other people, Schall says, all of whom he sees as dangerous creatures, and so he avoids all encounters with other people.

My experiences were quite different, and I recorded them. I saw him at night in Speyer. He wore a light, billowing coat. His movements were quick and of a certain grace. Coincidently, while I was in Speyer I witnessed the following event: in the glow of the streetlights, I saw him randomly meet a woman. They did not know each other, they had never seen each other before, yet they remained standing and felt at each other for a while, satisfied their desires, and continued on. They didn't lie down during the process. They had remained standing, and as this act came to an end, they broke apart without a word, he buttoned his pants, she pulled down her skirt, and they disappeared in opposite directions—without looking around, without faltering, detached as if absolutely nothing had happened.

Schall didn't describe this or a similar event in his reports. Schall writes: Reports on this man are still rather poor. He is indeed capable of blurting out muffled noises, and only raises his voice at times of greatest excitement. I believe it's possible to observe him for months on end without hearing a single word. He is seen rarely, and there is one exception, when he once walked toward us in the street, doubled-over or folded in on himself. If he comes across a puddle while walking, he crosses the street; he throws away shoes that are dirtied; his hands . . . what was with his hands? I don't know a thing about his hands, writes Schall. Schall writes: This man—if he happened to drop his hat—would not touch the ground, the floor. One of his idiosyncrasies consists of looking back when he walks, as if he wants to convince himself of how the things behind him look. He shakes his head, and then finds himself in the deepest state of reflection about the world.

This is what Schall says, and I won't argue this point. However, I must state a particular, absolutely true fact: Schall never wanted to observe the jerky movements, which I will touch on later. He reported other movements he was unable to put into words—but these jerky movements, which I'll touch on later, were something Schall never took note of. I noticed them, in a brief illuminated scene with a virtually naked female companion. At some point I will describe these movements extensively, but before I do so I'll describe something I call *The Fall* or better yet, *The Screaming Fall*. I'll describe the man on a roof with a woman; I'll describe their entanglement on the edge of the roof, and I'll describe how they keep each other company in a rather dangerous position, and how, during the climax, they fall, that is to say, they plummet from the top, they cry out as they fall, either from passion or fear. I will describe it with every available detail, with every word that is at my disposal. I can already say that this description will go smoothly. I'll bring everything else up later. For example, the unconfirmed rumor that this naked woman had something to do with Frau Schall. I'll come back to *The Fall* now and then.

Schall denies the whole fall incident. Schall says that this man often falls into the small, shallow rivers, whose banks he wanders during his nightly walks, but does so without faltering, and pushes on across the riverbed until he at some point reaches land again; then he continues his walk with a certain disinterest. As snow falls harder, Schall says, he lets himself get snowed under. In the summer he turns his face north, in the winter to the south, and in stormy weather he turns his face so that the wind can whistle over him. In his reports, Schall describes how, near Schleiz, this man sits quietly on the ground without moving. And when he walks on, he lowers his head to the ground, so that he appears much smaller than he actually is.

I repeatedly saw this man—whose name I can't recall even as I try—and was also able to observe him, how he goes out evenings, how he swings out of his window at sunset, with great agility—like an artist of speed. His movements were even, quick, fluid, and quite skillful. He jumps over rocky debris and easily climbs away over garbage bins, sacks of coal, and bottle receptacles. On the ground he glides, scurries. This man, I thought, is more agile than all the other men I've described. He walks along the street he sometimes takes, and walks no slower than the rest, but when he disappears he does so with astonishing speed—you can hear his speed, says Ramm. Ramm says: You can hear the speed.

You could only imagine my joy when, after all my attempts to learn more about this man, I met him on a cruise last May and had the opportunity to make a few new observations. This man found himself in the company of a woman—not yet mentioned by Schall—who, according to Ramm's findings, was a woman not only similar to Frau Schall, but who actually was Frau Schall. This is not mentioned in Schall's reports. And whether or not this woman really was Frau Schall, we'll never know for certain.

Naturally, this little cruise didn't allow me to dedicate my attention solely to him, this largely unknown man, in the manner I would have liked; but this brief time on the water sufficed to prove that virtually none of Schall's reports corresponded with the truth. One could hear the subtle whistle of the storm, the clattering of spoons, the soft lapping of the waves, the onset of music, the creaking of planks, the rubbing of bodies against each other as they danced, and the laughter of the sailors.

Back then, near Le Havre, I was able to approach him and succeeded in completing my observations. I will not claim to have established a connection with him. It was a short encounter, somewhat in passing, somewhat fleeting with a slight bow, and a few trivial words and nothing more. I could say: It really was nothing. I don't, however, want to immediately end what I've begun. Near Le Havre it became clear to me how dangerous it was to have this man around because he often used his dreadful hands in an undesirable way. He wreaked massive havoc and confusion on the ship, I remember it, as he propelled the majority of the sailors overboard, just because their laughter displeased him. He broke arms, ribs, and jaws with his huge fists; the sea churned on that evening—which had begun so pleasantly with the sounds of the water, the sea—the entire sea churned. I heard a soft thud, which I would say was like a crunch, maybe a crunch, and I saw swelling like I'd never seen before; lumps and deep tears down to raw flesh. He moved up and down with great speed and was, in all of this, the picture of extreme nocturnal excitement. However, as I quietly held out a pencil to him and asked him to write down his adventure, he instantly calmed down. He grabbed the pencil, apparently intending to assure himself of the specifics of the matter. The way he turned and twisted his head for this purpose exceeded everything I knew, and called to mind the fluidity of a pianist. The ease and dexterity of his movements, the swiftness of his decisions, carried me to admiration, just as his baseless anger frightened me.

We know Schall described this man's way of life in great detail, but, as we know, with completely different results from my own. When he stands, says Schall, all you see is the front of his head. By day he stands in the same position and appears to be sleeping, but as soon as a person or dog draws near he goes back inside. The sun leaves the window, and he goes ever so slowly back to his corner and, as expected, lays flat on the bed.

I have not witnessed this and I don't know anyone who has. Ramm didn't mention it. Ramm also didn't mention his allegedly short, ruddy feet, which Schall did mention. Indeed, his feet are small, but they're not red. Sometimes, according to Schall's detailed descriptions of his gait, he actually has a severe limp. But he takes leaps so broad that their breadth far exceeds the leaps of all other men in the world. He was praised for his serenity, politeness, and manners, but one shouldn't think he ever made friends with his observers. Schall is equally indifferent to meeting him as Ramm, or me, or the entire area surrounding him. If he has to eat, he doesn't worry about anything going on around him; every location is fitting to him and every region comfortable, especially around Schleiz.

Essentially, everything about this man is either odd or utterly insignificant. I can't comment on anything else. But I have no doubt that there could still be a lot left to describe in order to construct a complete picture. After all, the above records are the first attempt at such a description. Whether or not I ever touch on this subject again is questionable. I am able to claim that the man who I saw for the first time in spring interested me just like any another man I reported on in the past, but no more. And so I'll end here and move on to another man, though before ending, I'll title this report about the man from Schleiz: *The Laughter of the Sailors.* Would you please repeat that, said the man as he lit a cigar in Berlin. I said: What should I repeat. And he said: Everything, from the beginning. Everything.

No Story

I don't have a story to tell about an accountant's wife who was unable to sit because she caught a filthy, itchy disease. I've never heard of such a case. I also don't have a story to tell about the illegitimate birth of a child, on the occasion that the woman in question implored me *not* to tell the story. I have never in my life—and definitely not in a hospital—turned off an oxygen tank and then told a story about it. I know absolutely nothing about the birth of child with a frog-head, and I've never said anything about it. Furthermore, it is not true that I repeated a story to a group or several groups regarding the alleged comments of a man who claims that women wash themselves less and less. That I had, on the occasion of a woman's death, said I had a dark story to tell about her, is made-up and far from the truth. It is not true. The only truth is that every one of these stories was not told by me, but by a man about whom I once told a story, and in which I claimed that he had told a bad story. But that is not the point of this story.

On the Edge of the Atlantic Ocean

After an idea suddenly popped into my head, I took a piece of paper out of my pocket and wrote: A man yelled out in fear. Shortly thereafter, he died. That's basically what happened, in any case, generally and essentially. These last remarks admittedly went too far. Of course, the reader deserved nothing better than the waves crashing over the man's body, and the rain rolling in simultaneously, streaming down from above. Maybe he didn't even deserve *that*.

Disclosures from the Field
of Crime Fighting

While a mailman stuck some mail in a mailbox in Selm—near the Funne Stream, which flowed past shallow and silent—a man from Münster stole a small package from the mail truck parked on the street. The mailman, who was made aware of the theft by the local residents, tracked the man, caught up to him, apprehended him, and turned him over to the arriving police officer, receiving thunderous applause from the citizens of Selm. Knowledge of this little package's contents, however, falls under the code of postal secrecy.

In Memphis City Hall

For approximately two hours, a man spoke in Memphis City Hall to the assembled guests on the duties of newly elected mayors. After the speech, the audience thanked him and this man—the assistant to the governor of Tennessee—was presented with a medal of honor. Surprised, he read the inscription: *For exceptional merits in the craft of plumbing.* Here he realized that he had been speaking in front of plumbers the whole time. The assembly for newly elected mayors was taking place in another room.

At Nightfall

Last Monday I began to describe a man, who turned the corner of 82nd Street with a tremendous yawn. I didn't want to describe his yawn, in any case it's indescribable, and I didn't want to describe how he turned the corner, but rather, I wanted to describe how this man—or differently, differently. I'll start over, and with the following words: You can imagine my disappointment last Monday as I saw a man—not taller than Lemm, but about my height—turn the corner of 82nd Street, a man, a salesman, a salesman from New York, from a part of the city that's the darkest and most abysmal. No, that's weak, and not very good, maybe I should begin like this: A man about whom we haven't heard too much and who, based on his life to date, has done nothing worth mentioning, suddenly turned the corner of 82nd Street. It was a man who won't be discussed again in the future, or rather, who won't even be in any future discussions. That's better, but not good enough. My purpose is to describe things as accurately as possible; so I'm starting again and am describing a man who turned the corner of 82nd Street at nightfall. However, I won't describe this man's apparent horror. Right now I'm describing consequences, the consequences of his horror—or not that even. Rather, I'm describing a man who turned the corner of 82nd Street and approached me. This man held nothing against me, and in any case, he didn't voice anything that would suggest the contrary; and anyway, if we can accept that this man is more than a pale image in Lemm's mind—who had described a similar event—then we would be quite content. But we are not content, we want to know *more*. So now, I could describe the tip of his shoe appearing, the tip of his shoe, or his gloved hand, in which a revolver might be held. Or I could describe a hand without a revolver—that also would have been possible—or something completely different. I could describe the moon over Manhattan and the drifting fog. Perhaps I could describe the steam that rose from the sewer, from the drainage shafts on Columbus Avenue near the Museum of Natural History; perhaps I could describe the light that came on, on the 6th floor, and the windows opening, a person leaning out and the scream, which was so unique and inexplicable, I can say that I've never heard anything like it. But naturally, I could have also described something quite different on Monday, in Manhattan. And while I pondered it, this man I am trying to describe turned the corner of 82nd Street and said, I believe: *It's surprising that you don't remember me*, or he said nothing as he walked past me. It was like that: a man walked by and said nothing. He was silent like all the men who walked past me then. And while I thought over these correlations, a man turned the corner of 82nd Street. *Now that I've run into you, I'd like to ask you something*, said the man—who had suddenly turned the corner of 82nd Street—*and I don't doubt that you'll have an answer to my question.* In this moment I felt a tension for a reason that wasn't fully clear to me. The man gently nodded. He was probably in a hurry because he didn't stop, didn't exchange a word with me, and then disappeared. Or he disappeared after we exchanged a few superfluous remarks about the weather and how life in New York is becoming boring. From then on, I often saw the man turning the corner of 82nd Street. The pace with which we moved towards one another was not fast. Normally he stopped and said a few words, which, according to my memory, mostly regarded the state of his health. In the course of our conversation we must've had an argument, the matter of which I can no longer remember. Later, I didn't meet the man as often. Or to be exact—and naturally it has to do with accuracy—I have to say:

I never saw him again. Nevertheless, I could say a lot more about this man at this point. Perhaps my hat collection also belongs in the framework of this story, even though it has nothing to do with the man and nothing to do with 82nd Street, and absolutely nothing to do with New York. And what's more, I'm not even certain if it's the man I wanted to describe last Monday. All I know for certain is that I've never seen this man again. Suddenly, it grew quiet and dark. It was like this earlier, the weather before I started this story, not the outcome of the story itself: quiet and darkness. And everything I will now proceed to describe will overwhelm you with even more wonder than anything I have described up to now.

Along the Way into the Deep

A man, who was extraordinarily cheerful and lively considering the outcome of this story, said that he once traveled from Jena to Kahla by train. He had a good memory and a very round face, and would have hereafter remained an unknown person had he not suddenly made a remark in Arabic and talked about a way into the deep. I forgot the remark, and at the moment I am so indifferent to the way into the deep, that I will spare myself any further words about the way and the deep. The story, on the other hand, I am happy to tell.

The Next Story

The next story I'd like to tell I already told on Monday, and would not like to tell it again. So I'll tell the story from Tuesday. But now it occurs to me that absolutely nothing happened on Tuesday that I could talk about, so the next story should begin on Wednesday. Wednesday . . . what happened Wednesday? I don't remember Wednesday, and Thursday even less so. And Friday the least . . . Friday, Saturday, and Sunday the least. I don't remember any of these days, so I'll tell the story from Monday. It began in Olm, or rather in Ober-Olm, in the northernmost part of the city. In Olm there was a man, a cigar dealer, who was so disappointed with his life that he decided to move to another region. Upon arriving there, he came up to me and engaged me in conversation. The man said he had heard noises, as if someone yelled something like: *Help, help.* Then he saw a person, who yelled something like: *Help, help.* And next to this person he found a note on the ground—on the street—and on this note, written in almost illegible handwriting, was something along the lines of: *Help, help.* This man—named Netzenstein—who stood there, facing me and talking incessantly, was employed as a cigar dealer and was from the north of Olm. I haven't forgotten him, and will now direct my reader's attention to Netzenstein, a man exhausted by the stress of travel. Netzenstein told how he perpetually had unpleasant feelings, not only in the north of Olm, but also here, where my story takes place. For example: if he threw away a match after lighting a cigar in a tavern, he would have to go back later—in an hour or a day—to check if the tavern had burnt down. When he drops a letter into the mailbox, his disposition compels him to go to the post office in order to get the letter back, so he can tear it open and check what he wrote, and above all, to whom he wrote. Netzenstein said, that in Olm, or more precisely in Ober-Olm, he occasionally toyed with the idea of shooting a bullet into his body, through his urethra. Netzenstein closed his cigar store a half a year ago, and now travels around bars, frightening patrons with the specifics of his life in such a manner that they all flee from him. He eats alone, and said he does so gladly and with a healthy appetite, but he has a number of unpleasant feelings. *Encouragement won't help here,* he said, *I'm making a point of letting you know that it's no help at all.* He said, *absolutely no encouragement, and I'm asking you not to test me on this fact.* He walked out into the darkness and unzipped his pants. It is unfortunate, he said, that he has these feelings right now, where he used to have great plans and speeches. Once, when I walked with him along the Mosel, he suddenly screamed: *Away, away,* and jumped into the river. I'm drawn to the water, Netzenstein said at this point in my story, it wants to swallow me whole. He had to come to shore, and immediately. If I understand it correctly, he considered himself lost. At this moment I thought: Certainly this man feels things, touches them, but they do not make an impact on him. He's afraid of things that mean nothing; however, because he is surrounded by meaningless things, he will always be afraid of them.

In the meantime, I'd become quite accustomed to this man—I even benefited from his presence. Netzenstein certainly seemed to have no clue as to what he was doing in my story, especially at this point. As he stood across from me on Monday, he was a fat, somewhat pale, translucent man; I'd never seen a man with such a beautiful hat. He says he has to die soon, meanwhile his heart beats in his stomach, his nerves are already dead, and now his heart is being compressed, it's bursting out, in the air. During the course of the day

The Next Story

I had resolved to ask him something, but I no longer found the right words.

This man, who seemed to be all skin, suddenly cried out. The particular reasons with which I could have tied it all together didn't come to me. He cried out and began to stagger. His involuntary bodily movements—the shaking, for example, shaking and twitching, the process of breathing, swallowing, above all the swallowing—were unfavorable for the progression of this story. In the end, he was so fat that he wheezed when he walked. He loved oatmeal and over-ripe fruits, prepared as a thick porridge with near-raw meat, black and green plums, pumpkin, turnips, and kitchen scraps. His entire behavior was in no way human, though perhaps a bit swinish. Having said that, he was in the habit of becoming intensely terrified by unknown apparitions. He would back up a bit, trembling, and shut his eyes in despair. The first time he saw me, on a cloudy afternoon, he dropped to the ground as if he'd been shot, but then got up again and continued, without uttering a single syllable.

I believe he died from fright. A storm caused him distress. Seeming dazed, he immediately jumped at a flash of lightning, turned his ears to the rolling thunder, looked wistfully at his hands—wet from the rain and shaking from this tremendous incident—shook his extremely heavy head up until the moment a blow ended his life. This man, Netzenstein, was the uncle of the Honorary Consul from Honduras, who was greatly shocked over the outcome. He immediately cancelled his vacation in Stanz and appeared in my story. This sequence could have been entirely different.

51

The Mysterious Thimble
and the Strange Smoking Pipe

In a bush, a man randomly passing by on the night of April 11th noticed—no, a different beginning. A strange man, who to the best of my knowledge had never been observed, stood on an exit ramp on September 4th and at that moment pushed—no, no. Maybe like this: Maybe we'll look further back, at how a man named Schwill, even though his name says nothing and means nothing and it's basically wrong to refer to him, as a result of some unfortunate events and circumstances on October 3rd—not that either, not that. But maybe like this: On the early morning of August 10th, a man from Kiel was walking along a street when suddenly a second man appeared to the left of him. The man turned around and ran back the way he came. He must have been an innkeeper. Now two men appeared, and more and more men appeared; three men, four, five, six men, and so forth appeared. Seven men appeared. I'm unable to better articulate my statements at this time; I hold two things responsible for this: first, the novelty of the whole approach, second, the fact that the nature of these men, their professions, their family histories are completely unknown to us, and third—what was third? Anyway, I believe the reader has the right to know how this matter ends. And I undoubtedly have a few reasons for telling this story to the end, but I've just now changed my mind. I feel neither good, nor bad about it, only tired. At least there's one point made at the end that goes without saying. But there was something more I wanted to say. If only I knew what.

From the Secret Records of a Missing Private Detective, Which Were Found in a Shot-Through Briefcase That Had Floated Down the Rhine and Washed Up on Shore Near Neuss in the Middle of the Night

After we've started four or five times, we'll start again. It's no problem, we'll just start again from the beginning, it'll work. Naturally, it's not easy to start all over without important things like gloves, pipes, a revolver and a hat, but it's possible. We drive through Cologne, and it's the middle of the night. At that moment, a man in Sülz gets out of bed. A man in Kalk also gets up. More men get up. On this night, men everywhere get up. Just past Sülz we discover that a man got up there, too, just past Sülz. At this point in my report, no one knows where this man comes from, or where he's going. He appears and then vanishes again. We also still have no idea who this is about. He could be the victim, the perpetrator, the perpetrator's accomplice, or a completely different person altogether who has absolutely nothing to do with this case. I think it will all come to light—maybe as soon as in the following lines.

The Origin and Meaning of Sounds and Habits Which One Usually Doesn't Speak of and about Which There Isn't Much to Say

A man was in the habit of going for a short walk in the evening. On one such walk, he heard a noise behind him and, as he turned around, he noticed an unknown animal that immediately began to growl. About six weeks later, this man went to visit an acquaintance, where he met a large society of naturalists. During the general discussion, one of the naturalists ducked under the table, put his ear to the floor, listened for a while, and shared his findings with the other naturalists. He said it must be the growling of some unknown animal coming from beneath the floorboards. Everyone became convinced of the validity of his claim and immediately decided to burn the house down. The man excused himself under some false pretense and left the naturalist society. On his way home, he heard a noise behind him and, as he turned around, he noticed an unknown animal that immediately began to growl.

Moll

Not only is actually engaging with Moll—the man from Mörfelden—
awful, but even the idea of engaging with Moll is awful, so it's not
only the engaging with Moll you avoid, but also the idea of engaging
with Moll, says Noll. I don't know who Noll is and I don't want to
know, but I know very well who Moll is. I can easily imagine myself
traveling to Mörfelden and engaging with Moll for a while. Perhaps
I'll do it. But that brings up the question of whether or not I shall
write about Mörfelden. If I *don't* write about Mörfelden, then everyone will think I don't appreciate Mörfelden. And even if I do write
about Mörfelden, everyone will think I don't appreciate it. It's true, I
don't appreciate Mörfelden, but I do appreciate Moll. I already appreciate Moll because of his name. I like that name: Moll. But I don't
just like his name, I like his cheerfulness and I like *what* he experienced, and he's experienced a lot. For example, he never lost his
good humor when he suddenly sank into the deep Miami marshes.
He laughed loudly as he sank, and solely because of his laugh did
several people nearby show up to rescue him from this terrible situation. That was Moll.

Moll doesn't let a day go by without dealing with ordinary life.
He arrived in Reutlingen like a man of iron constitution: after lying
in bed for a while with a bread knife in his chest from an assault by
two muggers, he decided to ride his bicycle to the hospital, where
the knife was removed. The incident started when he had wanted to
have a beer on a park bench with a view of the Swabian Alb, when
two strangers approached and demanded two hundred Deutschmarks. Moll said he didn't have any money. And so one of the men

wordlessly stabbed him in the chest with a bread knife and disappeared. That was Moll.

On a night of a full moon, a man with an overall scruffy appearance was caught at a pretzel stand in Marl trying to stuff himself with pretzels; he had opened the window of the stand and helped himself to them. He had undoubtedly found himself in an unfortunate situation. A few hours later, on the morning of the following day, this man once again stood out; this time he had eaten a mettwurst in the grocery store. When he was confronted about this act, he fled, but was stopped again, and was this time taken into custody to prevent further offenses. There, someone found a small slip of paper in his jacket pocket, which made it clear that he was not without means. Whether the man's statement that he'd received the slip of paper from another man for safekeeping is true will now have to be clarified. Incidentally, that wasn't Moll. And Moll is not the man who squatted down to pick flowers, who floated downstream between Davos and Wiesen on Wednesday, who floated away across the small knoll, and continued to float away, floated across a grey and rocky field, slowly floated away, light and silent and literally unheard into the ravine, where he finally disappeared. Moll is also not the man who only wanted to stretch his legs, and while doing so lost his bearings, was hit by a vehicle and flung into the oncoming lane. That was near Bremen. This man, lying there, was suddenly illuminated from all sides, the body near Bremen this evening was completely white, completely pale, completely cold, and completely radiant.

The dark, unlit side of a body, of a person, of a man, was eventually discovered in Tulsa, in a lockable bathroom alcove in the American city of Tulsa, in northern Oklahoma, two hundred and thirty-three meters above sea level. A man sleeping while standing was found there. The public was met by a barely describable scene. In three years, this man had not washed or cut his hair, or changed his clothes. They found about three pounds of trash in his pockets that he had picked up off the ground. He had calluses on his feet three centimeters thick; his toenails had grown through his shoes. Ladies and Gentlemen, the man said, you are witnessing something definitive here. And that was not Moll, a fact we wanted to reassure you of, but rather a different man. It was Noll. Moll, at this moment, sat in a restaurant in Mörfelden and ordered another half pint of beer.

The Heart of America

In the heart of America, in the deep, overgrown woods, I met a man, a friendly local. This man was very fast. I believe I can say that he was the fastest man I knew, but with the exception of his speed, his movements didn't indicate anything significant. The only encounter that's important is the one I'm talking about. It's not easy to describe the encounter in a way that prevents it from being confused with other encounters. After all, it would be too complicated to list every comparable encounter. For example, Doctor Klomm, one of the first visitors to America, extensively narrates all of his encounters in the heart of America in such a way that one can barely understand why he received the Academy's badge of honor last year for his *Treatise on Every Encounter in America*. However, the reader already knows from other parts of my book that the case must be considered in the context of incidents that I never again want to discuss here.

As I left the heart of America, I decided to bring this friendly man back to Europe, alive, to showcase his speed; because after I'd gained some experience, it seemed to me that he would be particularly suited for testing in the field of speed. Although my expectations were met with disappointment, my efforts still acquainted me with his habits. Between you and me: after a short reflection, everyone who had seen him was completely convinced Europe had no use for such an indifferent man. His voice mostly consists of creaking utterances without expression or passion. He either remains lying in a single place, or he digs himself deep into the ground and disappears.

Naturally, I'm accustomed to these outcomes by now and, furthermore, now is a good opportunity for me to shift away from the roaring acclaim that isn't meant for me, but for an entirely different person, a certain Klomm. I'll sneak away, to the hot heart of Africa, where I'm welcomed by a great silence, a black, dismal silence.

Happy Birthday

We were just singing "Happy Birthday" to a man whose birthday it was. Suddenly I heard a bang; an explosion—someone yelled: Get down! And while we were lying down we continued to sing "Happy Birthday" to a man whose birthday it was—face-down, "Happy Birthday." And the man whose birthday it was said: What happened? And we said: Nothing happened, stay down. Then we took a bus down a dark hole and continued to sing that old standard. It didn't take too long, and we came back up into radiant nature, everything was all right. I said: Hopefully everything will stay like this from now on, nothing will happen, at least nothing that could be mentioned, nothing worth mentioning. Someone said: Why are you lying on the ground? Why are you singing face-down? But we no longer knew why we were singing face-down, we hadn't realized that we were still singing. We'd driven down a hole and later we'd come back up into the light and sang "Happy Birthday"—it could be, it's possible—and, of course, ladies and gentlemen, two hours later everything was forgotten.

Herr Korn from Kirn

I must confess that the records from my undoubtedly witty friend Collunder are incomprehensible. He wrote about Herr Korn from Kirn. However, neither the character, nor the life of Korn gives the slightest cause for a report. I assure you that I have never witnessed his quietness, as it is asserted by Collunder. Collunder writes that he throws his spoon up in the air when he eats—something I have never seen. He will eat anything that is soft enough. I would not want to call his gait heavy, as Collunder does. Not heavy, certainly not, but maybe Collunder's claims refer to a completely different man, whom I've never seen, whose gait I could never have observed; and if they do indeed refer to Herr Korn, then they cannot concern Kirn, but instead another part of the world. Maybe in the hard-to-breathe, contaminated air of the Asian forest regions, provided that they're overgrown, or in all the American forests, or the stripped-bare areas of Africa—but not in the clear Kirn air. As far as air is concerned, no region in the world, with the exception of the territories in tundra climates, is comparable to Kirn. As could be expected, Herr Korn from Kirn also says that walking in Kirn is like an airy gliding, a beautiful sailing along. I shared my observations with Collunder, and he promptly sent me the reports on another man, who plays a particular role in the road construction industry in Konz. And so I am content, and presume the reader is as well.

The Rate of Fame

In the past, Lemm was often compared to Klomm, to whom he absolutely shouldn't be compared because, one must admit, not a single feature of Klomm's can be found in Lemm. Enough about him, but think of him from the start as a man to whom there is no one to compare. So we won't talk about Lemm or Klomm. We'll talk about Hamm instead. Hamm, a connoisseur and aficionado of difficulties, the inventor of a processing machine, once became involved with various connections deep under the surface of the earth, was looted by a band of thieves, and almost butchered. This generated quite a buzz in research circles. However, it's known that there are no sources more abundant than the countless reports from travelers about the foreign lands they traverse, or in the dry narratives that often provide deep insight through few words into the overall nature of the world and its inhabitants. All scholarly claims, all their deductions from the highest principles of knowledge burst on impact at the simple facts of taking a beating and of stolen luggage. So said Hamm. He was soaked through and dead tired; and after several hours he had recuperated and become a famous man. That he was forgotten in the meantime is another matter.

A Glance at Life Last September

A man had bought a sausage at a bockwurst stand and ate it just outside the fence of my front yard, barely ten steps away from my office, where I was at the moment busy with my notes on subtle behavioral differences between humans. I looked out the window and quietly let it happen. As he bit into it, another man came up to snatch the sausage from him. But he grabbed it so forcefully that it burst and spattered into the air. This short observation was already sufficient to earn the man our pity. He deserves understanding and sympathy. It's different with the second man. Up until now I had not learned much about his life; it's just as nocturnal and unknown as that of one of his friends, as described by Wobser. Overall, their lifestyles seem to be so similar that it's good enough to describe just one of them. In their way of life, habits, their appearances and the way they move, dress, lift their hats, and the way they bite the tips off their cigars coincide to such an extent that, while describing one of the them, the other is also being depicted. Even though it's noted that one of them usually lives in the lower levels of buildings, namely in damp cellars, vaults, and sewers, or on a watergate or a riverbank, while the other chooses the upper floors of buildings, preferably lofts, garrets, and airy attic rooms, not much remains to distinguish one from the other. I took note of the situation and got up to check the soup. Good, the soup I wanted to warm up on my hotplate is still doing good. This story is still far from being over—I get the impression that it's beginning right now.

A Visit to the Left Bank of the
Rhine with an Unexpected Outcome

With the remark *I'm not doing so well,* a man came up to me and
fell over. That was last week in Kruft. It occurred to me that it was
as if he was covered in a layer of mold. I know I could tell this story
much better, more extensively, and more precisely, and probably more
beautifully, but right now I'm not in the mood. I was reflecting on
a completely different matter, which occurred in Mörz, but fine, I'll
remain in Kruft—I can try. A man, a butcher's assistant from Andernach named Dobauer, didn't laugh much due to a difficult childhood
spent in Kretz. He came up to me and fell over. The cities Polch, Bell,
Löf, Wehr, Ochtendung, and Niederzissen will be mentioned and
described in my story, which finally ends in Kruft with the words *I'm
not doing so well.* The man who spoke these words, a butcher's assistant from Andernach, came up to me and fell over. In this instant,
I thought that perhaps the story of America would have taken a
different turn if I had never seen this man; the story of America,
Africa, Europe, at least the story of this region on the left bank of the
Rhine—at least *this* story that I'm writing right now, in which a pale
man covered in a thin layer of mold suddenly appears and falls over,
appears and falls over. I'll try to reflect on it as little as possible, right
now, with the rustling pages of the Koblenz *Rhein-Zeitung.*

An Adventure in an
Oberschleißheim Pub

I believe it's not overly risky to explain what happened last year in Oberschleißheim. Last year in Oberschleißheim, a man in a floppy hat appeared. No one knows his name, or else they keep it secret. The man is from Röhrmoos, or he acts as proxy to a man from Röhrmoos, or maybe not even that. The story of this man, who passes himself off as a flat roof specialist and over the course of time actually talks quite a bit about roofs—not only about flat roofs, but also about hip roofs, pitch roofs, gabled roofs, shed roofs, half-hip roofs, and if I remember correctly, collar beam roofs, but most of all about flat roofs—is, however, not only the story of this man, but also of a completely different man, a man from Unterschleißheim who ripped a steel door off its hinges so violently in a pub in Oberschleißheim that chunks of plaster fell down. It all happened in a split second and was quickly over, a minute disturbance in normal circumstances, something that doesn't have to concern us anymore. So I'll now talk about Oberschleißheim in general. I've never spoken about Oberschleißheim, and because of that people believe I wouldn't want to talk about Oberschleißheim. That's not true, because at this moment, in which I'm aware it's important to talk about Oberschleißheim, I want to talk about Oberschleißheim. Naturally, it's only with great restraint that Oberschleißheim can be described as being important enough to talk about in order to talk about it. At least I didn't, under any circumstances, describe Oberschleißheim as important; at this time it seems that Oberschleißheim really is unimportant, and that every sentence, every word, even the smallest word, would be wasted on nothing. Oberschleißheim. Up until now, not many have heard

65

anything about Oberschleißheim and, as I've never talked about Oberschleißheim, I'm not going to start talking about it now.

Later, I was sitting in a pub on a hat belonging to a flat-roofing specialist. The dark and peculiar sounds coming from his mouth caught my attention. I waited for a surprised or outraged remark from the man whose hat I was sitting on, something emphatic, perhaps somewhat rude, but in any case final. Gladly, said the man on whose hat I was sitting: What would you like to hear?

A Remark on October 21ˢᵗ 1999

Excuse me, what prompted your remark, said a man as I approached
the reception desk at the train station hotel on October 21ˢᵗ 1999,
and I said: I didn't make a remark. I can't even guess if the next
man who shows up in line will make a remark. I also don't know if
my abilities are sufficient enough to describe this showing up, or to
at least prove my competence for such a description here, in front
of my readers. Anyway, I have doubts about my competence regarding the problem that surrounds and seems to occupy this man, and
from which he is trying to momentarily step away in order to get my
attention. Before I give any thought to this, I'll turn my attention
to another man, who's lying crumpled under the table with only his
feet visible. Without an extra explanation, no one would figure out
why two identical-looking men are behaving so differently; and yet
the explanation is very simple. You shouldn't wait for an explanation from me because I just decided to turn my attention to another
man. This man is resting his head on the table, as we can see, but in
reality it only looks like that, and has no bearing on the continua-
tion of this story. I am also not really interested in this man, but will
only compare him to the man I wanted to discuss at the beginning
and who is standing beside him—not directly next to him, but at a
little bit of a distance. If I were to hear that the man I mentioned
opened a door and disappeared, it would live up to my expectations
and wishes entirely, enabling me to easily turn my attention towards
several other men. They are men with a purpose, coming in as if they
invented their purposes in the moment they entered, and they are
in reality only meaningless purposes. Incidentally, all of these men

wear their hats on their heads, and, between you and me, that seems somewhat boring, but I won't dwell on it. Instead, I exhibit a certain interest in listening to a man whom I don't see, but can hear quite well. *Excuse me, what prompted your remark*, this man said, as I approached the reception desk at the train station hotel on October 21st. And I said: I didn't make any remark. That was '99, a rather shitty year for men—men who went to the brink of tolerability, the end of their strengths, men with hats firmly adhered to their heads, shoes firmly attached to their feet, men who did not have a solid grasp on what could happen to them in a train station hotel. And that's not nearly all. I'm refraining from describing what came next. I'll do everything to avoid confusing you with more words, I said that time in '99. I stood up. *Where are you going?* someone asked, some man asked: *Where are you going?* But I didn't pay attention to the question, I left, and refrained from describing the further development.

Important Remarks on the Basic Movements of Time and Place, of Feet and Legs

In November I saw the swellings of the city, its lobes and its blisters, overflowing with the slimy secretions of the sky, which had just split open; I saw an enormous, deep tear out of which they flowed. In that moment, a man tried to get my attention by saying a few words. It was Nagelschmitz, who, much to my surprise, had arrived in Cologne yesterday. I had heard that he had left Africa; according to the press, he should have arrived in Berlin not long thereafter—and under circumstances that are still unknown—wearing his famous, billowing, white coat. Nagelschmitz is an active person and a casual observer who has spent his entire life in a series of constant physical and geographical movements. He appears and disappears in the same moment. I saw him disappear from behind the Giant Mountains and from the peak of Montserrat. He rushed through the upper atmospheric layers everywhere, sometimes with his hat raised triumphantly. He raced through the world with unsurpassable speed, leaving only an unclear picture of himself. His face is virtually unknown. He jumps up and down with equal ease, describes curves in nature and disappears a little later into tremendous heights. It's a marvelous, silent humming overhead, I had noted in November. Other authors found different words, but I'll stick to my comment.

This man, Nagelschmitz, is a foreigner; all the writers are in agreement about this. There are those, however, who claim that there's nothing to say about him walking, that he's not even capable of crawling—they even claim that he's unable to stand up. However, as I can prove with direct observations, this is not the case. Look, noted Klomm: The man changes the position of his head, apparently at will, but it's normally in an unnatural state: it trembles. Noll, another author, claims that, as effortless as this turning of his neck is, it appears so cumbersome in comparison to his other movements. Every one of his movements happens at a speed so slow, you'd have to call them more than thoughtful. His slowness surpasses anything he, Noll, had seen in this region. As I gathered from Schwill's reports, he, Nagelschmitz, considered everyone with the same indifference. The heat draws him up from the cellar. Sometimes he lets out a sharp whistle, otherwise, according to Schwill's observations, he remains silent as a grave. His only wish and pleasure is to . . .

Schwill's reports end here, so I can continue on undisturbed. Occasionally—these are my words—Nagelschmitz sings at night, not very loud, and only at night. Collunder shares this view. The way he sometimes turns his face into the wind, it must mean he really enjoys air, that he eats air, he bites into it. His body sinks completely in large volumes of water, only his head remains visible. He doesn't avoid damp places; he walks around muddy banks picking up little fish. How many feet he has is unclear—sometimes it looks as if he has no feet at all. He also visits the edge of the bay, between the tightly compact leaves that provide cover, and walks silently along.

I reflected for some time on Nagelschmitz under the title *Important Remarks on the Basic Movements of Time and Place, of Feet and Legs*. At this moment I am content with the conclusion that the above-described man gets up and leaves the area. I don't know what his reasons are. Now, subsequently, I'll sit down and put everything in writing. I'll firmly compress this person and calmly arrive at the end. Afterwards I'll turn towards the city's swellings, its lobes and blisters overflowing with the slimy secretions of the sky that had just split open, and I see an enormous, deep fissure out of which it starts to flow.

A Little Further Up

A little further up a man arrived. The arrival of this man was a completely meaningless event that I hardly noticed. A man arrived, good, but it's such a minor event, it no longer surprises me. *You're not particularly surprised, I can see that*, the man said. Your appearance is nothing extraordinary, it's completely normal, I said. What this man said in return was amazing, but I wasn't surprised. A few years ago this might have amazed me, but these days, I'm never surprised. Then again, after all the experiences I've had during my long life, I don't find such stories to be as unbelievable as many people claim. *I'm incapable of seeing your point of view*, the man said as he left the bar. But it should get even better. Or even worse, that's also possible.

Everything Else Later

Max Ramm was around one hundred eighty-eight centimeters tall as he walked out of the illuminated gateway of the Natural History Museum; he held a heavy, black cigar in his slightly raised hand. It was Wednesday as he turned left, under the flicker of the neon signs, in the direction of Woolworth's. Concealed behind his tanned forehead was the intelligence of Collunder. His fists were more feared than Wobser's. His steps were faster and more determined than Scheizhofer's. All the women gliding across the street turned their heads to watch him as he'd pass, going into the Ambassador with the smooth, lithe movements of a tango dancer; a little while later he'd leave the shop, lighting a Havana. He mastered twenty-eight languages and his marksmanship was amazing. He was an orator of extraordinary caliber and, at the same time, was strong and silent. A relaxed smoker who had the regard of those well-traveled, who was a wine connoisseur, an art lover, and a master violinist. Max Ramm's hearing was as good as a bat's, his eyes far outperformed those of an owl, and where his physical strength was concerned, he could effortlessly lift the heaviest of weights with one hand, as many times and as high as he liked. Max Ramm was great, we won't argue that, but even better than Ramm was Paul Marix; he exceeded Ramm in nearly all aspects. At this moment, Paul Marix lay among the overstuffed cushions of his settee, in his silk housecoat, when his Chinese butler entered to give him news from Doctor Mowas. Marix opened the envelope, he slit it open with an ornate, valuable, Andalusian letter-opener and removed from it a mysteriously blank page.

Moments later something dark and thin jumped through the open window, through the softly billowing nighttime curtains. Something approached rapidly and with the words *Hands up, I'll shoot*, a man stood in front of the desk with a revolver-like object. Marix got up with his usual composure. I've been waiting for you, he said.

Marix set his pen down and looked out his office window. I'm happy I found my pen, said Paul Marix, and I'm excited about the paper that I found. I would start this chapter by saying: I'm happy to have found my pen. The lamplight cast a crouched silhouette on the wall. That's your silhouette, Mister, said Paul Marix as he shook my hand with great kindness. Everything else later.

The Nature Surrounding Prutz

In order to add a new twist to my life, I decided to go on a little walk one day. I hadn't gone far, when two men rushed secretively out from the forest's edge. It was so unexpected that my companion—the naturalist Schmädel, who was extremely agitated by this incident—felt he had been put in great danger. However, the aforementioned rushing out from the forest's edge was quickly forgotten so we could direct our conversation to another topic: nature. Thirty minutes later we found ourselves near Prutz and considered taking a detour to the famous ravine. Two men who obviously had the same idea appeared in the distance. However, we soon lost sight of them, and from then on we dedicated our attention solely to the sound and the smell of growth, the moss, and the constant transformation of the landscape. This relentless decomposition of the world, as Schmädel noted, the decay and erosion of the mountains, the masses of debris sliding and falling, sliding and falling as they disintegrated into smaller and smaller pieces, which he summed up in the word *detritus*. Detritus, he said, that is nothing more than what we see here: The rubble, sand, and dust surrounding Prutz. I would like to mention that, in this moment, as Schmädel talked about the complete absence of trees, two shadows fell darkly on the ground next to me and disappeared again. A while later, or a little bit later, we had taken one of the corner tables at the Gebirg Inn and ordered lots of boiled pork belly, when two men walked through the door and sat rubbing their hands together next to the cold, sooty stove. There was a lull in our conversation about the nature surrounding Prutz. Both men, who wore black suits, fell silent. Their silence was so conspicuous, so elaborate, that I didn't want to contradict Schmädel's speculations that they had something to do with criminals involved in dark secrets. Time went by. They remained silent, until the bartender in the background slapped the lid of a beer mug onto the counter in the vast silence of the restaurant, at which point both men got up and disappeared into the adjacent room. We went to the window in anticipation of even more dangerous events. Schmädel suddenly lifted his hand and pointed at two men in the evening atmosphere, who bounded like shadows down the main street and boarded a tour bus with their bags. Schmädel made another remark about the state of nature. I, however, was too distracted to consider it. In fact, I preferred to dispute Schmädel's remarks, and decided to go on a little walk, in order to add a new twist to my life.

The Pleasure and Pain of Berlin
and the Strange Effects
of Arctic Painting

Perhaps I should talk about Berlin now, about this slowly evaporating city on the edge of Central Europe, about the pleasure and pain of Berlin. However, I don't believe that there is pleasure and pain in Berlin. I don't believe there is a Berlin. And if Berlin actually does exist, then I can only say that it's completely superfluous to talk about it. Berlin is not particularly important, or rather: Berlin is completely unimportant, completely indifferent. Berlin is not worth discussing in comparison to the characteristics of Arctic painting. So I'll turn my attention away from Berlin and observe the far North, where I returned from a very arduous journey.

I described this journey extensively in my last travel reports. I began, if I remember correctly, with the words: One day I was up North, in the breathtaking cold, where I met Collunder, a man with a unique serenity and radiant skin who, wrapped in a heavy coat and wide-eyed, wordlessly recorded observations on the coldest place on Earth.

The fame, I wrote at the time, that Collunder has acquired as an Arctic explorer has lately seen a surprising increase due to the likewise great and well-deserved recognition given to the creations of his paintbrush. The number of his paintings is still admittedly small, but every one lights the way to mastery. One can safely claim that, next to Geselschap, Arctic painting has produced no greater representative than Collunder.

At the time, I took the opportunity to publish a cracking, icy image: the depiction of a single solemn moment up North. It was an image of numbness and dreadful frost that aroused a particular amazement, or rather, admiration, in every gallery in which it was exhibited. It depicted the exhaustion of a group of travellers and their seemingly imminent end: Prell, the photographer, looked with resignation at the hat he held in his hand. Glotz, the guide, had his arm in a sling. Behind him was the snow-blinded Englishman, Shepp, sitting with his eyes bandaged, and absorbed in silent despair. In the bottom left corner, Doctor Kepes can be seen lying in front of a leaking barrel, surrounded by his faithful attendants. To the right, standing at the edge of the photo next to Wobser, who's almost knee-deep in snow, is the cook, who had presumably come down with scurvy and was trailing behind the group on crutches. All of these men were, in some way, horrified to their innermost core by the reality the painter had depicted. Only Nagelschmitz looked confidently into the distance. For a while we searched for the man who had created the image, for Collunder; and then there he was in the moonlit background, blurry, but nevertheless recognizable. There stood Collunder who was not only taking notes on the scene just described, but also painting it. All in all it's a masterful depiction of this memorable journey to the North Pole.

Of course, if you consider how many groups have travelled to the area by now, you could say the subject of this work of art is actually quite common, but the execution shows such an original interpretation and such fine observational skills, that one must assume it comes from an artist who has spent a very long time in the cold. But you'd be terribly mistaken. Three years ago, Collunder received an invitation from the Art Academy in El Paso. He accepted this invitation and now enjoys the satisfaction of working as a Master in the same building where, years ago, he took his first steps towards fame as Tranchirer's favorite student.

El Paso is beautiful. In contrast, as I mentioned in the beginning, I don't care at all about Berlin. And so I avoid discussing Berlin.

Berlin is a slowly evaporating city on the edge of Central Europe that is perpetually striving to exhibit its originality in almost all aspects: in pleasure, pain and indignation—of course, especially the indignation over my personal opinion of Berlin, which I just expressed. In the meantime, the Berlin public will have formed its own opinion— which I unfortunately cannot share at this point.

A Man Wanted to Leave

A man wanted to leave and searched in a cardboard box for something important and essential for his departure. He didn't find it, but he did find something in the box which he'd long since been looking for, something that he needed to stay here, which is why he stayed and was happy things had turned out that way.

Awful Words

A man appeared and delighted us with the words: *I did it, I did it.* However, his words were much less pleasant the next time we saw him. He said: *I didn't, I didn't.* They were awful words that I would have gladly spared the reader.

One Day the Door Flew Open

One day the door flew open. A man bolted into a room, a man who has already been mentioned elsewhere. *Hands up or I'll shoot.* One could've expected as much. By no means has every relevant question been raised, but nevertheless a few have been.

A Short Description
of a Long Journey

Ladies and Gentlemen, I would like to kindly encourage you to devote your attention to this short travel account. You know from my publications that I stood up in nineteen ninety-seven. I departed and drove away with a small suitcase. The purpose of my journey has slipped my mind. I also don't recall if I traveled north, or south. I don't know what circumstances I left behind me. I believe everything I left behind changed, evaporated. I got up, I left, I traveled for a while through the outdoors; I got up and sat back down, then went on, and everything behind me began to change—I'm sure everything fell through or fell over or fell away. One day I arrived in the Congo, and I'll make a few casual remarks about that arrival, about my departure and about my arrival.

But first I'd like to tell you about a time when the only water to be found was what had collected in the footprints of elephants; I drank from them, in the middle of Africa, in the wavering heat. There were animal carcasses in the dried-out lakebeds, one on top of another in many layers—bloated, twitching, and rattling. The overlapping carcasses caught my attention in such a way that I made up my mind on the spot to produce an elaborate report. But just as I was about to begin, a man appeared in the background of this scene, in this deserted area, a man, who then immediately disappeared into the undergrowth. He appeared and disappeared, and everything happened so suddenly, that all I wanted to make note of was this event, this appearing and disappearing in the middle of Africa, this slight movement. I observed all the other things without a bit of concern.

Later on, east of Guatemala, there was talk about long, thin, ground-dwelling animals that would suddenly disappear into deep holes, never to surface again. That was a discovery I made near Mazatenango. I'll describe them in detail when I have the chance, I thought. I remember quite well that for a good while I thought of nothing other than these narrow, very moist, worm-like bodies that disappeared into the ground—but eventually lost my train of thought on this, too, and what's more, in precisely *the* moment in which a man silently offered me a black cigar. I sat near Mazatenango—that's the order of events—in a bar by the ocean, when a man appeared and sat next to me without a word. I thought it appropriate to reflect on that—not now, not in this moment, but after an acceptable pause. But another man appeared right during this pause. He appeared with an ordinary hat and an ordinary hand gesture. This movement, this hand gesture, was so ordinary that it, Ladies and Gentlemen, wouldn't surprise any of us. So I won't describe this movement, at least not at this time.

Shortly thereafter, I continued on without another word. Near Nagasaki, again in a bar by the ocean, I saw a man pull a fat fish from the depths. Perhaps I should describe how he sliced the fish down the middle while nodding his head. A giant, frozen moon hung over the procedure, a giant, frozen moon that I'll describe later. The slanted, tranquil flight of the night birds and the clouds of gnats, the gnatclouds, caught my attention. I wasn't entirely indifferent to it all, but indifferent enough for the moment to stop paying attention. Something similar happened in Rangoon and in New Orleans. In Calcutta my head was flooded and in Lagos, in Shanghai, in Yokohama, anywhere I sat and reflected on life, my head flooded.

An incident that I've never forgotten, and which I'll write down at some point, was the sunset in Valparaiso. The sun in Valparaiso set with such speed, with such force, that I rushed out of the bar and into the distance. I decided to speak about it extensively at some time or another. At that moment I only had the desire to rush out of the bar and to continue my contemplation in another bar, an inland bar, in Santiago or in Talca, or even better in San Felipe. I sat silent and the man sitting across the table from me also sat silent. He hovered over the food in front of him; he hovered over the pale, fatty chicken and inhaled it. Finally he got up, paid, and left. I had to follow him and begin a life of adventure in order to search for him, and to finally find him, two or three years later. As I sat across from him in a hotel restaurant in May '99, in Hong Kong or another part of the world, and as the heavy sea rolled, I believed that this moment was so tremendous, so unique, that it could never be surpassed. I saw this man eat. I saw this man, in Hong Kong or another part of the world, as he bent over the table and wolfed down everything that was set before him with all his might. And in May '99 I saw him suddenly throw his plate at the hotel wall; I saw undercooked, drooping noodles and small, slimy puddles, and gristly meat on the floor, and the rats swarmed over the leftovers with immense speed from all sides of the hotel with high-pitched squeaks, a rat-like scratching. As I ate my dessert, I heard the sound of little bones being gnawed, of something being cracked, crunched, crushed, and the hissing, the low, rat-like hissing, and as I ate my dessert and watched this scene—which I'll report on extensively at some point—the rats attacked one another and ate each other up until there was nothing left of them, in May '99. Later I ate a small, sweet cake that sat prettily on my plate like a small, sweet cake, and which was pretty like a small, sweet cake and which tasted like a small, sweet cake. In the mirror opposite me, I saw how I stuck a piece of this small, sweet cake into my mouth, but it doesn't mean anything anymore, it was—after watching the mouth that closed around the small piece of cake in the mirror—utterly meaningless. This image held so little interest for me that I was convinced that an exact description should never be made.

Once it had quieted down, once the musicians had left, once the waiters had swept up the remnants of the night, once some plaster had fallen from the hotel ceiling, I walked out over the sticky floor, through the swinging door, and through the deserted street into the city. Later I sat on the beach in Bilbao and my head continued to flood.

I had been sitting there for some time when someone tapped me lightly on the shoulder. It was Nagelschmitz. I was absolutely astonished to see Nagelschmitz in Bilbao—or where I was then, Tampico or Montevideo? I got up to greet him amicably, but I sat back down. What are you thinking about, asked Nagelschmitz. I sat completely silent at that time, in May '99. I don't know what I am thinking about, I thought.

Later, if not considerably later, I searched the upper Amazon region for him for an entire week, until I found him. Nagelschmitz said something, though I didn't understand him, and he soon disappeared from sight. I can, however, assure you that I immediately began to think about which words I could use to describe this encounter—truly, I had every intention of recording this meeting precisely, but was distracted by a new occurrence and decided to continue on without a word. As I continued on, I came upon a man who wanted to engage me in conversation. He talked about groats silently sliding and scratching down the intestines. I didn't understand him and kept going. A while later I passed by a man who talked about the devouring of unplucked birds, about sacks of fattened snails, and a lot of other things, but I couldn't understand him. In the next moment, I reached a beautifully overgrown spot with pleasant, bubbling streams, and sat down in a restaurant. A waiter appeared and brought me calf's head pie, neatly sliced—a nice, pleasant meal, still warm and coated with an egg batter.

All that was astonishing enough, yet I experienced something vastly more astonishing in the first-class compartment of the express train to Mainz. I got up and sat back down, and everything behind me began to change. I traveled through the countryside for a while, and once I was back in my apartment, I began to look for a pencil so I could write down everything, Ladies and Gentlemen, that I have just now recited to you.

The Consequences of
Human Life in K

The newspaper reported an incident under this headline in the area surrounding Koblenz, which I would have thought to be downright unbelievable had I not stopped near Koblenz during the time in question. That said, I was the chance observer of a terrible event, which I will try to convey here in the fewest words possible. At the time, the end of September, the following occurred: in Koblenz, or rather in Karlsruhe—that's more likely, so good, in Karlsruhe, in Karlsruhe, an old man, who I believe was seventy-seven years old, struck his wife, who was ten or twenty years younger than himself, two or three times on the head with an axe, badly injuring her. It wasn't a life-threatening situation, though. These axe blows at the end of September were presumably the result of an argument. In any case, that's what a supplier claimed; he was supposed to deliver a case of white wine to the couple, and had entered the apartment for this reason. He witnessed the act. A moment later he also noticed a cigar, whose embers set a sofa ablaze and was the cause of a devastating fire in Koblenz, or in Karlsruhe. Now I'll try to explain everything in order. Forty minutes later, three hours later, six days later, three weeks later, five months later, two or three years later. I don't know anything more, or else I forgot the rest. Considering my sudden, what's it called: forgetfulness? Forgetfulness, considering my sudden forgetfulness, I would like to note at least a few pleasant sequences, but mainly I want to leave behind a good report, which has at this time of course slipped my mind. Instead, a terrible report comes to mind, a report *so* terrible, that I wouldn't dare scare the reader with it and deter him from continuing to read—or worse, continuing to live. That's where things stand. Things were a bit different in Kiel. At the appropriate moment I would have several things to say about Kiel, a few words.

The Penultimate Story

The penultimate story offers little cause for hope. Around ten o'clock in the morning, a twenty-seven-year-old woman from New York tied up her Yorkshire terrier in front of a deli on the Upper East Side. On the other side of the world, a man, a certain Wischnewolski, woke up and jumped out of bed. It's been said that a thirty-eight-year-old clerk broke into his colleague's office in Hechtscheim and destroyed an office chair. According to statements from the fire department, the sofa in a pastry chef's apartment on Nordring started to burn from still unexplained causes. A missing mechanic was found sitting in the back of a bus. How he got there remains unclear. Around ten o'clock, an approximately thirty-year-old cook signed in at a doctor's office in Drais. He explained that he had woken up in a cemetery. The consulted authorities determined that the man is unable to provide his name, or his background. He's also unable to explain how he came to be at the cemetery. A motorist stops at an intersection in front of the crosswalk and looks with interest to the right, where an accident just occurred. A cyclist might ride by at this moment. Around noon, an unemployed insurance agent calls the police and demands they remove the garbage from his apartment; it was beginning to stink, he said he felt as if he were being plagued by the smell. A superintendent says an acquaintance suddenly hit him several times in the head with a hammer. Then this acquaintance, a toolmaker, fled—no one knows where to. A waiter lets a truffled turkey fall to the floor right before my eyes. In this moment I considered the idea that I must finally come to the end of the penultimate story. The whole thing is so over-whatsit, overwhelming, that all I could think about was Wischnewolski, who jumped out of bed. When I ask him what he does during the day, what he does for work I mean, he says he doesn't do anything, in any case nothing special. Once, he, Wischnewolski, tossed a traffic officer through the front window of a deli, where the officer lay covered in blood lying among the tender hams, the sliced sausage, and the slices of roast beef. Then Wischnewolski leaves—it's good that he's leaving, it's good that this is the last time I have to say his name: Wischnewolski. Wischnewolski leaves the story. It is time. It's Saturday, five o'clock. No one can tell what happens next.

The Forty-Ninth Digression:
Twelve Chapters from an Exposed Life

1.
The Start of New Conditions

My dear Ladies and Gentlemen, you are waiting for me to tell you something about my life. My life was uninteresting. My life was bleak, quiet and uneventful, and not really worth talking about. My life was as such: it floated by nondescriptly in minute movements, or none at all, from the beginning until this moment, to now, where I stand before you to tell you something about my life.

I come from a family of unsuccessful criminals, of solitary murderers who couldn't find a victim, unlucky thieves whose hands only dipped into empty pockets, of actors with colds who swallow their lines, bankrupt crooks, booed pianists, forgotten researchers, and desperate travelers traveling in the wrong direction. I believe I had three brothers, two of whom had already started their careers by tumbling down mountains. After my third brother had fallen down the mountains, I walked into my father's company; he was a distant person, sitting in his office at the desk, his head resting hopelessly in his hands. I barely remember him. Right now I don't even remember the type of business this company did. And I didn't make any kind of impression, neither in this company, nor in the second company, where I temporarily held a job as a warehouse worker. As a matter of fact, there are people who claim never to have seen me, even though I could prove that I'd been there for some time; however, under conditions that I'd rather keep secret. But because I saw no future prospects, luck, or peace of mind, I left as quickly as I could. I know that I stood at a train station and boarded a passenger train, I know that I traveled, but I don't remember where I traveled to. Occasionally, I looked out the window and thought: What am I doing here, why am

I traveling, why am I looking out the window when there's nothing to see. But I continued to look out the window and thought it didn't matter why I was doing it, I just was. Perhaps I should've put my hat on, I thought. What gives you that idea, someone asked. Well, I was just thinking about it, I said. Don't worry about it, look out the window, someone said. And I did; I looked out the window. The war was coming to an end. Someone asked: Which war. Some war. At the end of some war, I stood in the cold train station without a hat, without a suitcase and—I noticed—without a coat, in front courtyard between the remnants of smokestacks and the crumbling, windowless brick factory, in the empty, unlit station street along which I slowly walked to see where it went—what I referred to at the time as *The Start of New Conditions.*

In '54 I worked in several bars as an assistant waiter. Some claimed I sang from time to time. Yes, I sang from time to time, but only briefly and very quietly, and only in the darkest corners behind the coat check. I slept in a tiny room cluttered with stacks of furniture, on a slit-open mattress reeking of decay. Otherwise, not much happened. Sometimes I sang a little, it's true, but all I basically cared about was that I didn't drop the beer. One day, in March '55, I received a letter that said I should come to B, to Berlin. Come to Berlin right away, while you're still in this chapter. Take the express train and come to Berlin. So I got on a train, looked out the window, and was on my way to Berlin. And what did I see? I was prepared for virtually anything, but not for this, not for what I saw. It was nothing special, but something very different from what I had imagined. A short time later I left Berlin and decided to go into theater. And I did—I worked for a while as a salesman; I'd studied several dramatic roles and recited them with a certain passion as I walked up and back down front steps of houses, to the applause of the housewives who opened and closed their doors to me. In order to finally end up on a well-known stage, I turned to a man named Döring, a former character actor, who received me with the typical charitability of such occasions and all the depictions of fear that surround the world of the stage. I begged him for permission to recite my interpretation of Doctor Q. He listened attentively: Not bad, but, dear friend, you're unable to pronounce Rs, Döring said, and those who cannot pronounce the R will forever remain poor speakers. Listen to me: Rrr. Now practice that wherever you go. Stand in front of the mirror and speak with the strongest exhalation possible, but without the loud tone of the R, the tongue must float and flutter. Finally, after many months, I felt the slight buzzing of my tongue. At least it was a start. During this time I worked as a night porter in a hotel near the train station in Cologne. I practiced my Rs and observed the people who passed by. Several men walked in with their hats pulled down and their coat collars turned up; it caught my attention that they disappeared with their female companions and did not look back after I handed them their room keys. While I sat at the reception desk and practiced my Rs, I heard these altogether varied shouts: small, short, sharp or rounded, gurgling, or ones that actually appeared to endlessly rise and fall. At the time I referred to these shouts as "the outcry": *The Outcry*. I heard the outcry while I looked out at the hotel's rear courtyard, at the corrugated tin roofs, twinkling in the night. I practiced my Rs as I looked out now and then, as I said, over the ash bucket gently illuminated by the moon. I'll gladly recall the confident, smoking domes of the chimneys, the beautiful, softly curving gutters, the fire escape reaching up to the heavens and, down near the ground, at the edge of this scene, the mysteriously barred cellar window, and the remains of the foundation, the beautiful, swollen bathtubs, the snug boxes of bottles rattling in the wind, the squeaking or the creak-ing—how does it creak?—the familiar creaking of the carpet hanger and the soft flaps of the astounding garbage cans overflowing with abundance. I heard the outcry—as I called it at the time—the final outcry, and shortly after the whoosh of the toilet flushing in the shaft between the hotel walls, where, if you were to lean out your window, you could easily reach over and touch the window of the room opposite you.

Back then it seemed as if everything would continue on like that. However, I don't want to omit that everything changed completely. Some time later I traveled north. I traveled north to see the world, to board a steamboat, a common steamboat, and see the world. Someone had written me: Come up north, come as fast as possible. Board the next train and come up north, it's beautiful here. So I boarded the next train and traveled north as fast as I could. I didn't object, simply traveled north, and from that point on I was up north. One day, I met Seeler as I was on an escalator gliding down into oblivion. I found out, however, that it was a mistake, an illusion, that it wasn't Seeler at all who was gliding into oblivion. I breathed on my cold, clammy hands, the momentum of my memory had sent me adrift— no one stood at the windows. I was fairly certain I'd been wandering for a long time up north over the cracked pavement; I saw the buildings that had been mentioned, to the left and the right, the buildings that had been mentioned, and of course buildings that had never been mentioned, on both sides of the street. I heard the shaking of the elevated train passing by, the crash of vehicles colliding, and a sort of growling, a growling or creaking, and the sound of people, the voices of people, the words, the words. These northern people, I thought at the time, stand on their feet and never fall down. And if they ever do fall, it's never that bad—it seems like they're never bothered by it because obliviousness to falling down belongs so perfectly to this image of the north.

2.
A Gradual Expansion of Dread

Up north I was suddenly whipped back and forth by the wind. I don't take pleasure in talking about things that have happened and are now in the past, I don't like talking about them one bit; actually I don't talk about them that often, or at all. Admittedly, at this point I'd like to make an exception. I'd like to give a short overview of what has happened up to now, but an excruciating, black wind almost tore me from the ground. I saw the stools in the small café almost topple, I saw the curtains billowing, the tablecloths fluttering and the flying, the high-flying newspapers, the wind whistled like a light snore, but that's just a beautiful observation plucked out of thin air. In reality it was much less pleasant. The pedestrians who dragged themselves by held their hats to their heads, flattened by the weather's whirling and swirling. And I, who was thinking about something round, not entirely round, but almost round, nearly round—about the world, which I finally wanted to get to know—I was blown across a large section of the marina on this day.

I now remember how things proceeded. I began to talk. I've never spoken so extensively about it to anyone, about what just happened between the toppling maneuvers of cranes on this day in September or October. I looked out into the distance and saw a large piece of sky. To the right was the city I mentioned. There was nothing to the left, in any case nothing worth mentioning. Then the sea came; it came with an enormous smack and swallowed up the entire lower half of the city, up to the wall. It stopped a few meters in front of me in the park, which disappeared under the water and later turned into a swamp. In '58, before everything vanished, I could just reach out and touch the wall of the quay with my left hand. I touched the bridge. No more words. From here on I'll keep quiet, and I know what I'd like to say with that. I touched the bridge on this evening in—just a moment—in '58, boarded a steamboat and steamed on.

But maybe it was different. Perhaps I'm mistaken. Perhaps in '58 I was still walking around up north and wanted to finally go out into the world to see what this world was all about. It was incredibly nice: the weather was gorgeous, it wasn't raining and I was already gliding past the Helgoland lighthouse. By the time it disappeared from view I was on the high sea and saw nothing in all directions. The world was covered in blue water; everything floated around me and, naturally, I floated and rocked gently too, marveling at the secrets of the sea and the gentle whistling of the air, and the white-clad passengers walking on the promenade deck, and these small islands torn off from the mainland that I could observe from the galley hatch, where I was busy cleaning pots and plates. I saw the ladies laughing, lying on deck chairs with their legs spread, and the gentlemen bending over them and pointing into the distance. Every once in a while we'd dock at a port in order to see the sights.

Back then, in '58, someone, I think the ship's cook, said: Of the things in the north, the sea most resembles an incalculable, snowy steppe with alternating ridges and recesses. I recall the soft, silent slide into the unknown. For a while it went well. But now the steamboat began to sway and continued to sway harder, while the cook pointed to a pale strip in the distance. That, said the cook in the haze of the galley, is the sign of an inevitable storm that will exceed all expectations. He spoke, if I remember correctly, about a hole in the sea, and he wouldn't stop speaking. I saw the undoubtedly significant change in the color of the water, and there it really was: just like the cook had said, a large hole formed and gurgled in the sea like the drain of a giant bathtub. It doesn't happen very often, but now it's actually happening, the cook said before he was swallowed up, before he vanished with a long, soggy scream.

Done, done—no, moving on: the beginning. At this point in my life, I jumped overboard, broke a few ribs, spit up some blood, lost my watch, and hurt all over. As I resurfaced, I noticed I was floating in the sea. For four days and nights I drifted on a small raft and realized that the Atlantic, where I was drifting, was not as busy as I had assumed. Finally a steamboat appeared and took me on board. I was given dry clothes; I got up and continued the journey as an assistant steward. From then on, I occupied myself with cleaning the luxury cabins, or attending to the casually dressed passengers who paid no further attention to me once I took care of their wishes. I served cocktails and small hors d'oeuvres on silver platters as the ship began to lurch. The ladies' silk skirts billowed and the men's hats flew up into the air, but this didn't last very long because the ship sank with a terrifying noise, which I would describe at a later time. Everything happened without a word. The passengers sank in an instant; only *I* would be rescued by a steaming steamboat, and continued my journey as a member of the ship's band. Back then I was a drummer and I reflected on life. The foam sprayed me in the eyes as I drummed. It was warm for days on end, and I saw birds above me, zipping away. I thought: It's exactly the same as always, so to speak, for example. And while we played *The White Dove*, I imagined the sea was boiling: cooking like porridge, or like flat cakes, or like lumps, like dough in which the ships were stuck—completely stationary, or trembling only a bit, neither sinking, nor rising. The sea, I said to the pianist sitting next to me, is kind of like gelatin, don't you think? Suddenly, I was hit by a stormy gust and was blown overboard. Good Lord, I thought, now I'm going to drown in front of all these people, in front of these happy, casually dressed passengers looking down and waving at me from the steamboat. But that wasn't the case. As I floated away I saw the gentlemen throw their tennis rackets in the air, saw the ladies flutter a little in the wind, delicate and white, and saw the steamboat, which had just been merrily drifting along, be suddenly sucked down into an abyss; it vanished into the massive, gaping depth of an abyss in October '59. The sea opened its mouth, I later noted, and swallowed up the steamboat in a single, huge snap. Then a wave heaved me into darkness.

As the steamboat sank, I might have clung to a mast top that floated by, I don't remember exactly. So I floated there. The sea was very still. The air was quite mild. The sharks, which occasionally nipped at my lifejacket, couldn't do much harm. I felt fairly good given the respective circumstances. Indeed, the prospect of rescue was slight, but I would nevertheless be finally rescued, in '59, by an oil tanker that appeared in the distance. The captain waved his cap and I was rescued; I went aboard and took over the job of the machinist, who had just died from an unknown sickness.

The captain had barely shaken my hand when it began to storm. The rain washed the suit from my body and a row of barrels off the deck. I heard them rolling darkly behind me and finally splashing into the water as I descended into the ship's bowels, into the black belly of the tanker, into the steaming, pounding machine room, where I spent another part of my life.

I operated the ship's machines the best I could. I twisted small cranks, pushed buttons, and pulled up and down on levers that grew out of the walls. I tapped on the barometer and the thermometer, the ventilation hissed, the nozzles whistled and finally I noticed a rattling, a slight, steady rattle. At some point I went up on deck. There I met the captain—a broad, bearded man—in a state of contemplation. A wall of black thrust toward us. Only in the gradually clearing morning air could individual shapes be made out. Everything was bleak, a great bleakness. That dark mass, said the captain, lying northeast on the horizon is probably Siberia or Alaska. But he didn't want to commit to an answer. Moreover, at night, especially at night, he'd see a milky liquid drifting up to the ship, gradually surrounding it. He also spoke of the surface of the sea sleeping. Nothing could be done about it. Back then I experienced windless nights and saw the giant, cushion-like moon. One evening, in '59, we almost hit dry land. But I don't have time to discuss or describe it here.

I remember a rattling; I also saw the coast, always moving closer. The sea seemed to be rumbling. The wind blew from all sides. The sea hissed, I believe it can be called hissing. The entire event could be described in a beautiful and somewhat engaging way, and in detail, but right now is not the right moment. I clearly heard the sea gasping—gasping, that's it, that's the word—the gasping of trapped air.

For whatever reason, a food shortage broke out on the tanker, and while I turned rusty screws on wheels and coils I heard a low, intensifying tick: tick, tick. I forget the reason for this shortage; by no means did we travel through barren regions. Murders were somewhat common on board. No one spoke about the murders. One morning someone found three sailors cut to pieces. Someone also found the captain's bloodied shirt, baskets with chopped up, gnawed on limbs, and numerous skulls, among which was the head of the unlucky cook, who had just told me his life story the evening before. I saw fewer and fewer movements in my surroundings; a depletion, as I noted in my reports, a complete lack of people. Only rotting bodies floating in the sea against the sides of the ship.

Finally—I believe in mid-December—while I was busy with the necessary course calculations, the overheated machine room exploded. I was launched out in a tremendous jet of oil, in a giant ejaculation. And as the burning tanker sank, I swam away.

An object that was miniscule in comparison to the vastness of the sea loomed beneath me, on the floor, on the sea floor; I could easily see it and could have grabbed it had I wanted to. And maybe I wanted to grab it, but in this moment, in this discrete moment in December, a small, sturdy ship traveling through this part of the ocean for the purpose of science and research appeared on the edge of the horizon.

I imagined the captain—a man named Töpfer, who greeted me amicably once on board—to be a traveling explorer; a meteorologist intending to make a sea voyage to the end of the world, to the point where an enormous thicket hangs down from above, and everything behind it is frozen, everything is smooth, a colossal smoothness, crisp and cold. Anyway, I had truly reached this particular point in December '59. I had set out to travel north. I wanted to go north, and now I was up north. As soon as the wind died down, the sea froze instantly, and as soon as the wind picked up again, the fresh ice broke apart. Töpfer said: That's just how it is up north.

Captain Töpfer, who didn't seem bothered by my presence, showed me quite an extraordinary electrical phenomenon on the horizon. The air was cold. Our hands froze in our pockets and their contents froze in our hands. We did not take this matter lightly, but we also didn't take it seriously, not *too* seriously in any case. There was certainly no hope left. This situation is hopeless, said Töpfer. And it was. Moisture condensed on the rigging and dripped down like rain. Everything iced over in such a way that walking and standing became difficult. The excess built up into a giant icicle, which would have fallen at the slightest tremor and pierced someone's head. In the distance we heard the squeaking of rats.

Then I wrote down the following sentence: Around 80 degrees latitude, the rats had bred to such an extent that nothing could be saved from them. They devoured pelts, clothes, shoes, the beds and blankets, they devoured the provisions, they devoured the entire ship and went under; they sank, and while they sank they continued to devour and breed. The dogs that had been brought on board to kill the rats had also been devoured—their howling could be heard in the fog before it became completely silent.

Then I stood alone on a piece of floating ice a meter thick, around 80 degrees latitude in the middle of the night. I bent over the rigid paper and wrote down an entirely incomprehensible sentence.

3.
Return to the South

I had barely finished this sentence when a magnificent, festively lit cruiser appeared, heading south with a costumed traveling party that beckoned to me with a bottle of champagne. And as I boarded, into the midst of amusements, I rediscovered the mood of years past, or rather, in trusting the improvement of conditions and in the hope for better circumstances, I not only rediscovered the mood of years past, but also discovered an entirely different, new mood. Before the cheering crowd, the cruiser went past one of the coldest places in the world in a beautiful, foamy curve; it is a place that has been given more than fifty different names over time. And because the ship's doctor was in bed due to a long-term, schnapps-induced stupor, I took his position; I became the ship's doctor, and from this point on traveled south.

For a while I listened to the singing of the travelers and the sailors' choir, the popping of corks and clinking of glasses. In January, I found there was actually very little to preoccupy my immediate attention; I simply observed the vast swelling of the moon; it swelled with great speed, which filled me with neither amazement, nor dread—as was later written, at that time it filled me with great concern: that's not right. A milky fluid surrounded the dark disc of the moon. It didn't disturb me at all. I was fairly indifferent to the black knots at the moon's edge, the knots at the edge of the moon, and to the foam on the moon. The moon doesn't rust, I thought, then said: *The moon swells, but it doesn't rust.* At this time I still heard the sound of corks, the spraying from champagne bottles, and the creaking in the cabins, the sighing, the thrusting gasps, gurgles ascending from the belly, and the muffled cries, and the rushing of the endless, black Atlantic Ocean.

I'm here because of a particular matter, said a soft, wan woman that evening, as she stood at the railing next to me with her hair billowing. She spoke about what had happened and what could still happen, and said to me: *If I fall into the water, Sir, please pull me out.* I will, I said, don't worry, I will. She resisted feebly as I began to unbutton her raincoat. Shortly afterwards I fell asleep, and as I awoke I noticed that I was floating, rocking peacefully, up to my armpits in water. And the moon was there again, without any real reason. The cruiser had sunk quickly and silently. I later learned that, when the ship had come into contact with something hard jutting from the water, only the silverware had clattered. Then I was alone again, somewhere near Africa or America.

I didn't have to wait long, however, because a cargo vessel appeared on the horizon and took me aboard. *Who are you, Sir?* the captain asked as I stood on deck, dripping. And when this cargo vessel went under, all I know is that I floated slowly through the tepid water and was fished out by a freighter. Shortly after, that ship began to sink. *We're sinking!* screamed the helmsman. It was nothing special. A fishing cutter pulled me out; I lay for a while between the fat bodies of the fish, and as the cutter silently disappeared beneath me into the Atlantic, all I wanted was to touch the sea—in '60, all I wanted, if I remember correctly, was to touch the sea, but the sea was long gone. I lay wet in the hold of a tugboat, on cabbages or potatoes, I don't know—on beans or bananas, I don't really know anymore—but in this moment they began to roll and I rolled with them, and as the tugboat sank in the background of this scene I slid into the water. What a life, I said to myself. I wouldn't ever say that under other circumstances, but now, where I had suddenly slipped into the water and resurfaced with my pants completely soaked, I said: What a life. I didn't say it very loudly, but I could hear the words: *What a life.* Then I tried, if I remember correctly, to simply float on the brackish surface of the sea, between the seaweed and the remains of the tugboat. Beneath me, in the deep, must've been the bottom, the sea floor. But I still recall that in that moment, I asked myself how I could've thought that this could be the sea, the sea, the ocean, the Atlantic, or as far as I am concerned, the Pacific Ocean. The sea floor wasn't visible, or, to put it better: not even the sea floor was visible.

4.
A Short Moment of Peace

At the start of chapter four I caught sight of land, which I walked up on and, later, in the fifth chapter, left again. I was in either Africa or America and had already seen much of the world, but everything I had seen was possibly less important than what came next—in what I believe was '61—at the edge of the world. Suddenly I had land under my feet. In front of me lay a box of something, and behind me I saw the sea. I took note of everything and wrote about a tremendous solitude, in which I found myself in '61. I also wrote about the sea. Naturally, not everything I wrote was untrue, even though I destroyed my notes a short while later. Only this sentence remains: *I have the impression that I'm at the edge of the sea in Africa, or in America, maybe even on the edge of the Pacific Ocean, or somewhere else; but it's unnecessary to waste a single word on it.*

I had walked mutely onto the land and sunk into the sand. I believe the wind stood still, and the sun? What was the sun like? I decided I'd record all of it in detail some day. I had walked mutely onto the land, lay silently by the sea and waved with a hat I had found on the beach—back then I found many hats on the beach, four, five, six, seven hats. I waved and eventually a steamboat indeed appeared, with a dark, round blow of its whistle. I noticed the distant dancing and promenading on its deck, but no one paid attention to me; no one noticed me. It could have been that I wanted to record something and actually did write it down: A steamboat, I probably wrote, that didn't respond to my waving. Around evening I lost sight of it. The sea was emptier than I'd ever experienced it to be. No more ships, and not much else apart from that.

I lay there for days without seeing a ship. But then I saw a whole row of supple, swollen steamboats that didn't respond to my waving. They seemed to lack human activity, were apparently without a crew, and no passengers, steaming along empty, outbound, gliding, smoking, or possibly burning, or rather, already long since burnt out and simply finished.

After this event, I searched for a distraction and began to explore my new surroundings. Fortunately, there was a library: seven hundred books washed up on shore, and as I read and read, the ground I read on sank inch by inch. I saw the small tips of islands growing out of the water, which disappeared, then emerged, and disappeared again. In the end, only a single tip jutted up out of the salty surface; then the sea vanished into the seabed, and the seabed opened, it burst and disappeared into an even greater abyss—all of this considering the facts I've quoted and recorded.

Quite an odd occurrence, I said as I walked onto land, still reading. This same thing occurred again the following day. Finally, in May or June, I felt tremors in the ground, and the next morning I saw a dark, dangerous object between the island points. By midday the water was quite hot; I heard a clap of thunder under the surface of the water. In the afternoon, the beach slowly began to sink. At five o'clock I looked to the east coast: an enormous blaze that was gone again in an hour. The ground shook incessantly. Something rapidly increased in size and then finally burst.

I didn't yet have the impression that I wanted to talk about or record something; however, I did write something as a result of a strange force. After having closely considered the event, I wrote that the island expanded like a bubble, and that at night it resembled a large pile of burning coal. The sea is a vast, thick pulp, I wrote, enclosed by a glassy mass. In my opinion, I thought, and wrote: *In my opinion.* Then I opened up a fish and drank water out of it, which suddenly brought on a new thought.

Nights like sausages, like long, coiled sausages. And days like hard, colorless grass. Sunsets like wide, silky, raised underskirts. Great, pubic hair-like shrubs, or at least arid, thorny tumbleweeds, and prickly beach peas. The vegetation was sparse, the ground occasionally scratched and wobbled. I began to imagine my bed, which stood motionless in the train station hotel back in Europe, at the other end of this story.

Dusk settled in the clouded sky around five o'clock, and the twilight animals could be seen approaching in large masses. They drew closer from the distance with a wet, congested hiss; they crept slowly from the mud with their twitching snouts. I wrote everything down, and then hurled bricks into their teeth, which cracked like lumps of sugar in their tremendous, powerful jaws. Upon slitting open one tumor-covered body, I found an undigested, chewed-up dog's head, pant legs, the feet of smoking tables, hat hooks and cans of beans, suitcases, cigar cutters, women's purses, vacuum hoses, handlebar grips, can lids, oily birds, broken pans, trampled eyeglasses, shattered bottles, sailors' caps, and overshoes without soles—all undigested.

The following year I had a momentary feeling that I was suddenly seeing blue smoke rising through the bushes—steam. And as I drew closer, the sea came into view, and I saw a group of men in the distance trying to pull something out of the water onto shore: something wet, laughing, not at all very big, and completely naked, loudly crying out.

That was the moment Captain Korn and his men came to shore, with whom I had stayed for several months. In their company was an unclothed woman, a vacationer from Berlin who will play a small, frivolous role in the next chapter.

5.
A Conversation about Seaweed

In '62, about a year after I had set foot on solid ground, several unexpected people appeared and enlivened this scene which was initially devoid of people. I'll skip the next lines of my report; I'll skip them and continue on to another page. I also know, I wrote, that we shook hands amicably and began to reflect on life. I spoke of the future, while Korn recalled the past—a time before his arrival in this part of the world, where I'd been since '61.

One day, for reasons I don't want to mention here, Korn left the ship with part of his crew; at the sight of a small, smoking island, he left the ship that was entrusted to his command and made for land. Shortly after he turned around, he noticed that this ship, this steamboat from Bremerhaven, had disappeared. All he saw was some smoke in the distance, nothing else. Korn talked about the wetness and hunger they had endured from that moment on. All that had grown on land was a parsley-like herb, but it tasted nothing like parsley, and the bird meat had been rancid and bland. Korn recalled he had found several suitcases, but they were empty; even the cartons and sacks he found were wet and empty, as were the dresser drawers he pulled out, the cupboard doors he threw open: empty. Every house, Korn said, had been empty, and the streets he walked through were also empty.

A couple of dark, unknown figures appeared here and there in Korn's story who wanted to speak, or who attempted to do so. But he, Korn, didn't hear, or didn't understand anything. So he assumed that these people had been inhabitants of the island, experts on these surroundings, who used their expertise to remain silent.

From my notes, I learned that Captain Korn spoke of unpleasant experiences; he spoke of layers of rubble and mountains of ash, and of fatal burnings. Or, for example, of the gradual disappearance of his companions, who suddenly toppled into chasms, or sank in mud, or who, simply being exhausted, were left behind in the wild. Just imagine: one second I'm just talking to them, Korn said, and the next they're falling down around me and in front of me. For instance, Korn recalled a particular Monday. On Monday around one o'clock in the afternoon, I saw, said Korn, a big, fat cloud. Several days before I'd noticed tremors in the earth, but they didn't arouse any special attention or concern because here they're natural, they are, said Korn, part of a normal everyday life. But on Monday they were so strong that I had the feeling it wasn't just everything moving, but that it was everything collapsing, as if a great amount of ash had fallen on me and I had to brush myself off. The island had, as I realized later, completely burst apart, and more than half of it sank into the sea. The sound from the bang circled the earth three times, Korn said in the description of his unpleasant experiences, conditions, discoveries, and occurrences, in his descriptions of various cloud formations, intense puffs of smoke, and the ultimate collapse. I ask myself, said Korn, what the public knows about this. It can't be much.

At least a female vacationer from Berlin—who Captain Korn met in a holiday flat surrounded by magnificent palm trees—had been a pleasant discovery. I will skip over the next few pages of my report. I will especially skip over a small, frivolous scene that Korn described in great detail: the vacationing Berliner's nakedness shimmers through the lush shrubbery, she's heard laughing and singing. Korn sees the lady and the rest of the crew in an extremely vigorous entwinement. Korn described every detail of this scene, and while I skip over his descriptions, they're followed by a conversation between Korn and myself about seaweed, which I will also skip. Eventually

Captain Korn reports on the ravenous woods that knocked down those passing through and quickly grew over them. Once, Korn said, we watched with horror as the water actually turned green from the leaves of a certain lurking forest that was hidden below the surface of the sea. At the end of Korn's report, only a sailor's outstretched hand could be seen protruding from the black, boiling, murderous mud. That, Korn says in my notes, ultimately spoiled our stay. He said that he assembled the rest of his crew, dedicated themselves to the sea, and arrived at the place where I'd been living for a year—in Africa or America, or some other place in the world.

6.
The Anaconda's Smile

At the start of chapter six, on a cloud-free, storm-free, wrinkle-free day, the missing steamboat from Bremerhaven appeared, riding smoothly and happily on the horizon, and took us aboard. Captain Korn asked me to be his guest, and to conclude my sea voyage, which started in chapter two, as a first-class passenger. I accepted his offer with great pleasure and lay down on a freshly made bed.

Occasionally, I looked out a small, round cabin window and was amazed at my sense of tranquility. I'd been lying here for nearly a week and was starting to feel sure of myself. It began to rain and stopped raining. The ship began to steam and it stopped steaming. It got dark and it grew light. The moon floated by. The sky's pelt thickened and molted. Something slipped in front of the sun and slipped away again. Where am I, I thought. Then I wrote: Where am I. Probably somewhere near 20 degrees latitude, in any case, somewhere at sea, generally speaking. At this moment there was a knock on the door and there appeared the smiling face of the vacationer from Berlin, a lounge singer. How are you, she asked. I said: I'm well, thank you.

The next morning I awoke from the pressure of an immense body, a soft, smooth, cool, gradually creeping body. I had already heard a lot about deadly embraces, during which even experienced travelers lost their lives. I recalled another morning in another place, and this memory does not belong to the enjoyable moments of my life. In the dull, moonless nights of chapter four, I often had the feeling that I was lying on snakes, as if I'd wake up on a layer of smooth, sluggish bodies in chapter four that began to move. It seemed as if the ground beneath me was slowly crawling. And something else, another memory. One day I jumped over a black, muddy pool, I stepped on something living, on something slick, spotted, and breathing; I was knocked down and before I could get back up, I felt something incredibly long and thick wrap itself around my body and begin to squeeze me. I was truly constricted so tightly and quickly in the fourth chapter that I barely had time to let out a slight groan. I heard a sharp hiss and saw something like a flattened head swing back and forth in front of my face; a putrid stench blew on me, I felt my ribs bending under this terrible embrace, and I assumed I was doomed. But things turned out differently than I had expected.

The singer from Berlin slid out of bed and crept quickly out of my cabin. That afternoon I lay on a deck chair on the promenade and let the steward serve me rum punch. I saw the singer from Berlin in front of me, bent over the railing, her wide skirt blown up at that moment by the wind. And as I looked down into the depths, I remembered another afternoon. I remember my constricted voice and the indescribable joy when someone, I don't know who, used a machete, I think, and severed the smiling head from its body with a single blow. The headless body still held me in its grip for a while, until it was cut through in more places. I heard cracking in the fourth chapter, the felled head was still snapping at everything the tongue touched, and the chopped up pieces twitched and jumped until nightfall. I finally felt a certain relief, but, covered in blood and mucous, I could neither stand nor speak. The length of the snake—as far as I could try to guess after its mutilation—was about five or six, I don't know, around seven, eight meters; the thickest part had the circumference of a common pig. For a long time, I couldn't forget the impression this adventure left on me. Not only the sight, but also the mere mention of snakes left me pale and shrieking. I was certainly of the mind that this couldn't continue. And that's what happened: it didn't go on like that.

At the party onboard that night, I saw the singer singing, gliding through the salon, and dancing out the exit in the arms of the captain. Engrossed in my memories, I walked through the mild sea air. I saw passengers intently groaning into and on top of each other, foaming at the mouths, and a black body slowly creeped out of the forest and began to draw me in, into the swamp. As I cut myself free, as I simply chopped up the body into numerous pieces with a machete, I was lucky to find my hat and said: There is no point in staying in this place, I'll leave now, I said. In the fourth chapter it crunched—I'm not entirely sure, branches cracked, it's possible, and a few drops splashed, could've been. All in all, in the sixth chapter, I no longer wish to think back on it.

Someone who wanted to tell me something about the sea passed by, and told me something about the sea. Do you feel the sea?, someone asked. Do you feel it under you? That's it. That's the sea. You must feel the sea.

Yes, I felt it. I felt the sea under me. For a while I remained silent in order to ponder the strangeness of the sea, the singularity of the sea, and not just the entire expansiveness, not only its width, but its depth, first and foremost. I said a few words in conclusion. Then the wind pushed my voice back into my mouth as the singer floated through the salon in the captain's arms, and continued to float out the exit.

I remained silent for a while, perhaps for a few hours or longer; I remained silent for a few days. We coasted by Charleston and still, I remained silent.

At this point, near Charleston, near the coast of South Carolina, someone wanted to tell the story of a woman at sea, of a singer; he wanted to describe how this woman used the movements of the sea, the rocking up and down of the sea, to enhance her pleasure. Someone said that she'd first sit on the First, then the Second Officer, and a little later on the head steward, the ship's doctor, and the steward, and she'd enjoy this rocking motion with great pleasure. Someone wanted to describe the outcry to me, the outcry or the groan, this woman's final groan, or perhaps the groan of the entire world; in any case, in this part of the world near Charleston, someone wanted to describe the swaying—the swaying of the ship, the swaying of the woman, an incidentally not entirely clothed woman, and, as it seems, the swaying of the whole world. And I remembered in this moment that this woman also sat on me once, with a soft, wan, almost flowing face, with wide-open eyes, transfixed, looking out over me, or through me into the distance, with an open mouth out of which came a distant breath; not a breath, but a wind, a wind-like sound, a deep, guttural exhalation, and breathing faster and faster, in and out in time to the swaying, with the rocking motion near Charleston, near South Carolina, with the scent of laundry—the pungent scent of laundry detergent and disinfectant. Why is this woman sitting on me, I thought, and I also thought: She reminds me of a woman in an underground parking lot in Stuttgart, and the smell of exhaust fumes, of depth and airlessness, of a woman who hit the windshield and yelled something. I thought: Why is she yelling, why is this woman sitting on me. I looked at her swollen face, she yelled something, but I couldn't hear anything, then she kicked the car a few times and yelled into the smell of gasoline, of floor polish or seaweed—seaweed? Yes, seaweed. And suddenly in the fourth or, I don't know, the fifth chapter, suddenly a, yes, suddenly a terrible hiss, a churning, a deep bubbling, an inward gasp, a sudden tremble, a series of circling movements, screw-like turns—what does turning a screw sound like? Right, so after a series of twisting movements, she vanished without a sound. She was no longer panting as she left my cabin without looking back. I heard her leave; I heard her open and shut a door, and open and shut another door, and there she began to yell, she screamed. I'm positive that I have never before heard such a substantial scream. Afterwards I forgot almost everything I'd wanted to say. I'd even forgotten if I wanted to say anything at all. However, it was already necessary to say something.

For example, a few words about the afternoon outing to a narrow cliff island, which emerged from the sea one day, would have been appropriate. However, had I known what would happen to me on this island, I would have certainly refrained from this little outing. Undoubtedly, it was the strangest memory from this journey, which was so rich in memories. But right now I have no desire to talk about it.

I was brought out into the wide, unpredictable world; I was mercilessly driven away by a relentless storm, was tossed around and pulled into the abyss with force. I didn't linger in the deep for very long. Later I arrived in a crackling drought, in a scratchy, waterless land that rubbed me raw. I saw someone standing coldly between the mountains, but that belongs in a completely different context, in another part of my notes. I had experienced and forgotten quite a bit and no longer thought about it. And now I was about to be happy, here, at the end of chapter six.

And so, at the end of the sixth chapter, as a singer from Berlin passed by laughing and disappeared into her cabin with the ship's engineer: Let's be calm, let's stop talking. Though I knew, naturally, that in this world you can't be calm for a single moment. There is no entitlement to being calm.

7.
Arrival, Departure, Disappearance

We arrived in Montevideo in the spring. I shook the captain's hand and left. I disembarked and was employed as a truck driver for a while. We arrived in Casablanca in the spring. I left the ship swinging my cap and earned my living as an excavator in the Moroccan mud. We arrived in Valparaiso in the spring. I went on land and cleaned display windows. The ship landed in Hong Kong in the spring. The crew dispersed and I disappeared into the city center and became a porter. In the spring we arrived in Rio, Bilbao, Bombay, Brisbane, Cape Town, Porto Alegre. I said goodbye to the remaining crew and became a soup cook, a stoker, an iron bender, and for a short time— only for a night—a bouncer at a nightclub, a news vendor for two nights, and a wrestler for about thirty minutes. In the spring, I set foot on solid ground in North America. We had arrived in New York, where I went on land and vanished into the crowd.

In Halifax I worked as a solo entertainer, but without noteworthy success; the audience didn't pay any attention to me, they paid, and left. In the London fog I stood at a small table at the weekly market and sold a cleaning agent. But no one stopped. No one listened to me. I talked in between the vegetable stands in front of me and behind me, while I rubbed the rusty hotplates, and the crusty pots and pans with circular motions. Sometimes I raised my voice and heard the core concept of my speech: *The most persistent grime,* I heard, *but also water spots, and with a wave of your hand—no more residue, Ladies and Gentlemen.* I didn't look at my movements, or at the pots and hotplates, I didn't look at the faces passing by, but stared into the fog. With every week the pots grew darker and the hotplates blacker, but I continued to rub and polish. I believe that was at the weekly market in London, or in Le Havre.

When we landed in Melbourne in the spring, I jumped eagerly off the gangway and mingled with the people below. There I passed the time until nightfall, in the spring of '64. I lay in a bed for some time in a hotel in Melbourne, or somewhere else. Thunder cracked in the distance. The time came when I had to dress in warm layers to keep from freezing. I knew from before that this time is customarily called *winter*: Winter. I also recall that a lot of snow fell in winter of '64, during this time called winter. Later I sold newspapers until the descending darkness prompted me to find my hotel. I looked up at the friendly moon. Suddenly, a new thought came to me and I wrote it down it immediately.

I had just started to consider my reports as important, meaningful, and necessary, when another thought came to me. Was it actually in Melbourne that I woke up in a small hotel, got out of bed, and took my leave? Melbourne? I became contemplative. At the height of this reflection, I boarded a bus and departed. *I suppose you would like to know where I am now*, I said to the man sitting next to me. *I'd go so far as to say that you'd like to know who I am.* But the man had no desire for conversation: he leafed through a newspaper, looked out the window, would have nothing to do with me. Then I heard a shout before I disappeared from the area.

Everything became cool and quiet. I noticed that the bus flew down a small hill at high speed. I was surprised that the winter I had spoken of had not come—the snow, the ice, and the frost. It remained as it was. I wrote: Nothing is changing. And later, after this entry, nothing changed. I ran through the pouring rain, between heavy, dripping trees, and didn't know what to think. It was certainly a new discovery I absolutely had to record. And I still had more to record.

I wrote a few lines about the almost-forgotten time before the incident. A memory of a boathouse in California wafted up, of a spruce thicket in Maine, of the beaches in Carolina, of the crashing waves in Massachusetts. A wan, shadowy apparition silently dances over the gleaming parquet; it dances through the wide halls, through the swinging double doors; it dances out into the gentle Missouri night, it whirls around and dances down the terrace steps in Texas, or in Tennessee; it dances through aisles in Minnesota and down stairs through the countryside of West Virginia, and through the heavy shrubs in Illinois, and back through halls and halls and halls, and through immense rooms whose names I don't remember; over illuminated squares in Alabama, and silently down the wide stairs in Pennsylvania.

A woman who sat behind me on the bus reproached herself for having come to this forlorn region. I wrote this down. We spent the night together near Tulsa. Then we got up and went in different directions with the intention of never seeing one another again. I hardly remember what happened. I only know that she cried out; she suddenly cried out here in chapter seven. She was—I recorded— almost naked under her coat and crying out. A white, slightly curved belly, I wrote, I saw this strange twitching movement, her tongue caught between her lips before her cry; I saw her black gloves, her garterless stockings, the long, pointed heels of her shoes—and I wrote down everything, I reported everything. The tip of her tongue suddenly tickling my neck. *What now?*, she asked. It was nothing. I barely felt it. Something spurted out of me, something burst—it was me, and something cried out, but that wasn't me. Something leaned back, something pressed its lips together while something spurted out of me.

Later, I made a new discovery. I wasn't ready for this discovery, but even so I wrote it down, and by the following night I had already lost my notes.

What is that? someone asked.

I believe it's a body.

A body? That's right, a body.

8.
Traversing Africa from One End to the Other

I don't know exactly at this moment, in the eighth chapter of my reports, if I'm in East or West Africa. I only know that I was a traveler who tried to cross the Dark Continent from one side to the other in '65 and in '66, and to whom it didn't matter from which side his venture began. I had intended to do what no one before me had succeeded in doing—to traverse this region alone on foot, and to make a series of interesting discoveries that I would take notes on. I wrote down everything that caught my attention. I took pleasure in these notes; to me they seemed to become increasingly important, they were the real reason for my journey from chapter eight onwards. I didn't write down my experiences, but tried to experience what I wanted to write down, in order to lend a uniqueness to my notes that has not yet appeared in literature, or at best not in in Scheizhofer's writing.

It's true I didn't traverse Africa for scientific reasons, but solely for my own personal pleasure. I began my journey with sturdy shoes, suitable head coverings, and, from this point on, was ready for anything. For example, in one town I saw animals as big as cattle and animals that looked like cattle lying in the sand, or leaning on tree trunks and sinking slowly to the ground while moaning. However, the tenacious grip on life that these animals had was so great, as Scheizhofer mentioned elsewhere, that you could cut and sell slices of them in the markets until only a motionless, yet still living piece remains.

The bodies of water I came upon on my hike were covered with a layer of slick slime, a reddish-green skin that was thick as a finger, which I pushed back purely out of curiosity, whereby a swarm of small, stinging flies rose up and attacked me. I ran away, I simply ran away—where to I can't say with certainty. Up, down, to the left or to the right, I saw a black flock of birds rapidly descending on me as a I ran across the sparse land, across the arid, scratchy, prickling earth. Swarms of giant insects flew after me and rows of caterpillars crawled toward me from all sides as the sun sank beneath the horizon, sinking with colossal speed. I saw a forest within reach, and in an hour I had reached the first row of trees; I entered the woods, panting, but then the ground under my feet gave way—the ground slid away on all sides. I lost my way in the darkness of the woods, I lost all ways, but that essentially didn't matter—besides, I didn't know where I should run, I ran and continued to go deeper into the swampy, muddy land; I became entangled in vines that wanted to pull me down into the gurgling depths, and I became tangled in snakes that wanted to pull me up into the trees so they could crush me in peace. I stood up to my belt in water, and then I felt a trunk, a tree trunk in my hands, and my happiness increased, but naturally it wasn't a trunk—as you can imagine—but a giant crocodile that I had climbed onto, and naturally I wasn't happy anymore, even though I narrowly escaped its snapping jaws when I jumped into the darkness.

I described the stale smell of the putrid puddles as I continued to advance in the darkness and grew accustomed to the idea of the swamp devouring me and my notes. I felt for my matches, and when I struck one I saw the small, dark, boiling, steaming pools of mud and the intertwining tangle of bearded and pelted trees. I also saw a spot that appeared dry, as gnat clouds swarmed around me, settled on me and covered me like a teeming crust; and pale maggots crawled from my body, out of my festering sores. I climbed onto the dry spot in this debilitating, airless humidity, but this spot began to move beneath me; it jumped back with a strange, steaming hiss, a wheeze, and a crack. To the right, to the left, the whistle of the mysterious bog monster, the crunch, the breaking of bones, the screams of my companion—a man I never saw again—I'm being crushed, the man screamed, his whimpers could be heard for quite some time, then everything was quiet: even the crunching, the breaking, the whistling, the gurgling, the munching, and chuckling had stopped. I wanted to shoot, but where should I shoot in this darkness, and more importantly, what could I shoot with since I had lost my rifle long ago. I'd used up my matches when a storm broke out, the kind that only break out in these ports. A hissing storm with water falling so heavily from above that I'd never seen anything like it before, nor would I see anything like it again in the future. It wasn't rain, it was just water, nothing remotely rain-like, only heavily falling water, and a hot pulp fell from the sky, and snakes fell from the sky, they fell, slapped against my body and crawled away as day broke.

Meanwhile, I found a horse and rode over everything in my way: the swamp, the forest, and the vast, dry plain, the humidity, and the drought. But then I reached an utterly barren place that was drier than the dryness described by Scheizhofer. My horse and I sank into the dust, we pushed on through this dust, and my horse kept sinking under me into this dust; at the very last moment I came upon a windblown and rocky landscape. The animals stared at me with their bloodshot eyes, with cracked or torn lips, their open mouths snapping at me, but it was a motionless snapping; their pale, swollen tongues hung limp and feeble from their mouths, and I still recall how they watched me sorrowfully. The region I later reached was cooler, the inhabitants friendly, and everything turned out well. I wrote down what I had experienced and finally fell asleep.

As I awoke, somewhere in the middle of the continent, I saw the wide-open eyes of a woman with a dark complexion as she sank to the ground in that exact moment. I lifted her up and tried to communicate to her through my gestures that I meant her no harm. But she tore herself free and ran away. *You want to go?* I called, *Then go, but I advise you to stay.* This woman ran away and began to disrobe and dig a hole with great speed; she disappeared into the hole— a very deep hole, from which gasping and panting could be heard. I didn't quite know what to say—she had disappeared yelling, yelling, or perhaps singing? The rainy season began. The sky covered itself thickly, and in this half-gloom, in the solitude and dampness, I wrote a single sentence that I later completed: *A felt-covered sky.* Afterwards, an unusual incident occurred that I would like to ignore at this time. At the same time, a storm slipped into this chapter. For a moment I was compelled to end my journey right here. I don't remember the exact reason. I stood still and sat down in chapter eight, in '65 or '66.

My life wasn't spared the consequences of rain. My jacket was wet. The tea grew moldy. The sugar absorbed water. The tools rusted. Giant black, white, and red ants crawled out of the ground. Worm-like millipedes scrambled out of the bushes. Above me hung the nests of numerous yellow-headed wasps, which were as dangerous as scorpions. Massive beetles the size of full-grown mice rolled from one side to the other across the ground. *If things don't change*, I wrote, *this will end badly.*

Some time passed.

Some more time passed.

Now, I was met with a sad sight. So sad, that I could've never imagined it possible.

Thankfully, some more time passed.

Finally, even that passed. I saw myself, in '66, standing in front of a thicket of acacias—no one had any idea of where the thicket ended. Not even Scheizhofer, who I met in this place on this continent, and whose expedition I joined for a while. Only someone of Scheizhofer's stamina and determination was in the position to even think about continuing this journey under the current conditions: creeping from clearing to clearing, and anyone who strayed from the path was inevitably lost. Fatigue claims its victims: someone lagging behind was bashed to bits by natives, a worm-related illness broke out, and, over the course of time, friendly people transformed under the sun into their grim counterparts. Anyway, the closer I got to the other side of the continent, the more beautiful and cooler the area became. Everything grew in abundance and the people I met lived in peace.

In the meantime, I had seen, experienced, and undergone so much, that I often had to refer to my notebook in order to refresh my memory on the main events of this difficult, grimy route. I remembered dried fish, oxen, potatoes, flamingos, swollen beans, molten rock, sighing trees, and, of course, the people who had made preparations to eat me. Large, indistinct men shook my hand extensively and warmly. Without a doubt, I had survived many hardships, but my journey—from what I could infer from my reports—was without question both substantial and useful for research.

Additionally, I was convinced for the longest time that I was on the road not only for my pleasure, but for an entirely different reason. I believe I had started my journey, if I remember correctly, in order to liberate a man named Scheizhofer from the control of African rogues. However, to my greatest horror, I didn't find Scheizhofer, only his remains. *I am curious as to who will be next*, I wrote at the time, *but no matter who it is, we can't change things*. According to my conservative estimation, there lay about two thousand kilometers between me and the sea at this point. I saw a lot, but the food was just as bad for me as the heavy, humid air pressing down on me. Even the instrumental music that kept me from finding peace at night was not among the pleasant impressions of chapter eight.

I left the area in March. I went even further east or west, through pits of debris, clumps of bulrush, and swarms of ravens; I saw thin, hornless cows with large droplets of moisture on their snouts, rises, dips, foaming abysses, dry rivers, and occasionally bananas and wire. I traveled through great secrets and vast riddles to the edge of this land without seeing the sun over the forests—and no one wanted to follow me, no one. Walking was a painful strain: crawling, grasping, struggling through the steaming jungle at terrifying heights and depths. But that was just the beginning of the horror. The entire journey was like a creeping fever, a mucousy congestion, and after all this creeping I was nothing more than the slimy discharge of my own head.

My shoes tracked through soft scat, disintegrated into damp pieces, and were completely eroded from my feet. The leaf lobes sank slowly in the mealy night. Everything meant something, everything had meaning: cracking necks, watery swells, the fat, festering corpses of plants, the cadaveric smell of the hairy bodies I crawled over, and, most notably, the crawling itself had meaning; the sticky crawling among the other creeping movements, among all the other living beings that crawled by me, under me, through me and over me, up my pant legs and out my sleeves, in my pockets, my pants pockets, and—only to give you an example—when I reached into my pocket to pull out a tissue, I'd grabbed something silky and crawling. Later, as I reached the destination of my journey, I was occasionally accused of exaggerating. Everything I had written down was lies, fictitious, pieced together in the most natural manner. Nevertheless, the success of my expedition from one end of the continent to the other, to the edge of this land, was finally recognized and honorably mentioned by Scheizhofer himself.

Meanwhile, my notes filled several volumes. I thoroughly recorded everything I saw in the countryside so that I could give a faithful depiction of its general characteristics. The outcome of this journey, as one can easily believe, was richer in experience than the collective whole of my past journeys, richer in experience than any journey undertaken by anyone. Richer, for that matter, than Scheizhofer's journey—with all due respect to his achievements. I like Scheizhofer, but Scheizhofer knew where he'd been. I hadn't. I didn't know, at any given moment, where I had been in this country, in what direction I was going and on which side I finally arrived.

The deliberate meeting with Scheizhofer took place, incidentally, with great mutual satisfaction. When I look back on my journey, nothing that I might've done wrong comes to mind. I believe I did nothing wrong. I didn't let anyone catch me off guard, no one, not even Scheizhofer. I traveled around this way, without being surprised. In short, I believe that by now I'm a fearless traveler without the delicate mannerisms of a homebody, who digs himself into a cozy hole in the world just so he can feel comfortable in it. That is my opinion on the evening of the tenth of December, 1966, at the end of chapter eight.

9.
In Konz. In the Hotel

I assume it's likely that, on the next pages of my reports, I'll leave Africa to continue life in another part of the world. Mind you, the notes from '67-70 are missing. I can't find them. This period remains dark and empty. In '71 I occupied a hotel in Konz, on Merzlicher Strasse. I sat at the window in September and recorded everything that caught my attention, and I will quote these notes in the sequence in which I found them.

I believe there are rooms I have not yet entered, even though I've been living in this hotel for almost a year. For this reason I went on a short walk yesterday, which I'd like to briefly describe because it's a pleasant memory. I left my room in the attic around 19:00, crossed the hall, passed the laundry room, the broom closet, the ironing room and continued on, left past the toilet, and down the staircase. It was a beautiful September day. A gentle east wind carried fresh scents over the earth, recently watered by the thundershower. Through the clean window, a vineyard lay shimmering before me in the evening light; to the left, the restaurant *Schons*; to the right, at a somewhat greater distance, but still close enough, was the plastic factory, and parasols in the foreground, the opening and closing sunshades, the terrace lamps, the lawn chairs, and all the way back, on the edge of this scene, the wonderful rivers gently flowing into one another. My path led me continuously deeper into the lower levels. I had already left the washroom, the shower room, and the breakfast room behind me, and now I stood in a small lounge, in the haze of heavy, black cigars. I dropped into one of the club chairs and looked through the panoramic window at the hiking trails in the distance.

I was surrounded by the sounds of pleasant conversation and the soft, foamy, flow of beer from the taps into the mugs. And as I blew smoke out of my mouth with great enjoyment, I got to my feet in an excellent mood and walked on, through the music being played, past the kitchen and the chopping of the cooks, past the scent of women's coats in the cloakroom. I soon reached the hotel restaurant and then the final place I wanted to go: the end of the hotel where I had lived for several months, the swinging doors, the exit, Merzlicher Strasse and Konz, the city of Konz. Here, I was without a doubt at the bottom floor. Of course I knew that there were other rooms beneath the ground floor: the boiler room, the wine cellar, the storeroom. As dusk approached, I sat back in my room and ate the ham sandwich I had brought. It was almost 20:00.

Or it was different, different. I left my attic room around 19:00 because of a silence that suddenly broke out. I didn't hear a thing, not even the rattling cough of my neighbor, a professor emeritus who had been coughing in the neighboring room to the extent that it seemed like he was pushing his body out through his mouth, piece by piece. I didn't even hear his cough, just simple silence, a very ordinary silence. I got up, crossed the hall, passed the laundry room, the broom closet, the ironing room and continued on, left past the toilet, and down the staircase. In front of me, in front of the window plastered with dead flies, sat small, broken televisions, cut-open living room furniture soaked through from the rain, lamp stands, shattered flower pots and half-eaten creampuffs. I continued my descent. There was nothing to hear, no sounds, not the howl of a vacuum, not the tinny movement of the cleaning bucket, not the splashing and wringing out of the mop, not the rolling, shaking and groaning of the washing machine, the smacking and gurgling, not the slamming of doors, not the hiss of the radiator, not the noise of the shoeshine machine, or the warm babble of water running in the bathtub, not the rush of the shower, or the pounding of feather beds and goose-down pillows. My path lead deeper and deeper to the bottom floor of the hotel, where there was nothing to hear; not even the clatter of type-writers in the office, not the ringing of telephones at the reception desk, and no voices: no voices. Not the receptionist's voice, not the voice of the porter, not the voices of the waiters and waitresses, not the whispers of the staff, the maids, the valets, not even the voice of the hotel manager. As a matter of fact, I also couldn't hear the cooks chopping in the kitchen, the chop, chop, chopping. An immense soundlessness. And as I sat in the small salon and looked silently out the bird dropping-spattered panoramic window, with its flutter-ing, soot-black tulle curtain: nothing, no sounds. The movements in front of the window: mute. The serpentine train in the distance, the passing trucks, the buses, the buses that pushed past, the buses: silent. The silence of a helicopter over the vineyards. The black, inau-dible swarm of birds rushing past the window, the inaudible sound of plaster falling through the air, of bricks, of rafters and bricks fall-ing through the air—all an outrageous silence, nothing else. There was no lifting of a piano cover, no sounds of conversation, no guests laughing out loud, no forks clinking in the restaurant, no forks clink-ing or knives scraping. None of that. No windows being torn open, no rolling down of Venetian blinds in the dark evening. No music, no singing, no applause. Just a simple, unabashed calm. Only the drops from the beer tap, the hard, dry drops of beer falling from the tap onto the bar. Only the sound of—that's right—only the sound of smoke being exhaled, cigar smoke, exhaled from my mouth. Only the sound of my breath and the rattling of the iridescent flies on the panoramic window, and absolutely nothing else; in fact, I got the impression I was the only guest in this hotel, the only guest among the torn-up wallpaper, the overturned stools and the silently swing-ing doors.

In the next section of my notes I again try to play a certain role—as an actor in my present state of mind. I had spent a good while figuring out where this iron door on the other side of the hall led to. I finally figured it out and could describe it in detail if I wanted to. But I've decided on another possibility, on silence, the wordlessness, the wordlessness in Konz.

My notes break off at this point. I only found fragments of my '71 report: loose, occasionally illegible notes, and I don't know which day they concern. Undoubtedly, I was still in Konz and I remember a massive silence. Only the sound of my feet could be heard, the creaking of the floorboards in the hallways, the hallways, the hallways. I continued on past walls plastered with posters and the creaking climb down to the bottom of the hotel, and then back up to my room. The weather was normal, like the autumn back in '59, which I already described in detail.

In October people appeared everywhere; I felt like they'd emerged from the walls with small suitcases, and raincoats, with bare, hatless heads. They didn't pay attention to me, and I must confess that, in all my life, I have rarely felt as unpopular as I did in that moment. Thankfully, the moon rose in Konz in October. In March, I didn't know what I wanted to say. A man, a professor emeritus, found me in my dark room, deep in thought. This man, who lived next to me, walked in and said, with great difficulty, as his body flailed about from coughing fits: When I was your age, no one would have found me deep in thought in a dark room. Go out into the world, to Africa or America; get to know real life. It was an evening that, although I ended up violently vomiting afterwards, remains one of my best memories.

I reflected on how things should continue now, at this moment in time, and as I contemplated this in Konz, in the hotel, I decided to keep my personal life a secret for the time being. Nevertheless, if

I allow myself to talk about myself here and there, then it's because I am still living—I wrote in March '72—and that the moment this life corresponds more or less to my expectations. For example, I try to remember something, but I don't know what I was trying to remember. I believe I overcame something, but I no longer remember what it was. Maybe I didn't overcome it. An unknown reason had driven me to Konz, to a hotel. So there I sat without a satisfying answer to my question: What should I do now, in March '72? I heard the sputtering cough of the professor emeritus living next door and decided to suspend my reports for a while. Maybe later I'll touch back on Konz and this hotel, where I will sit by the window and finish my notes, these notes that I have written with such ease, without making the slightest sound, without conspicuous pen strokes, and with great speed.

10.
The Society of the Informal

There are no further reports between '73-75, no further clues about my conditions, circumstances, situations, vocational activities, relationships, friendships, enmities, desires, opinions, and intentions; there are no clues as to my wishes, my adventures, my experiences, the places I stayed, nothing—nothing from '73-75, not a word or even a whisper, absolutely nothing. I first re-appeared in '76, in Bad Orb, in my reports on Bad Orb and '76, with a gun in my jacket pocket. I temporarily called myself Schubacher, and wrote the following:

I am happy I found a pencil, even though I wasn't looking for it. I am excited about the paper I found; I'll take this pencil and paper and begin the tenth chapter with the consideration that I am happy about being able to start a new life in Bad Orb under the name Schubacher. Here I shall establish the primary aim and reason for my new appearance, which—and this will probably be forgotten in a few years—occurs in a time of unrest and confusion. As a result of the deterioration of public conditions, I have decided to face everyday criminals and become a private detective.

One of my first assignments was to discreetly observe the Society of the Informal's annual conference. This conference held a heightened significance because of several members in attendance, whose names are still received well today, for example: Thiersch, Maßmann, Malitz, Dietz, Ennmoser, Bertschi, Scherer, Beck, Lachner, Pechtl, and Zumbusch. The chairman, Doctor Fischer, began with a preliminary address. He spoke—I quickly took notes on a substantial part of what he said—about need, namely about the need to more precisely follow the sun's movements, and the light expanding from it, the light, and the efforts of the Americans, mostly with the application of Wobser's old proposals, often with only minor amendments to Wobser's proposals, actually, in part with improvements to Wobser's proposals. Furthermore, he talked about sound, sound that wouldn't travel in the way that it does through the air in ordinary speech and conversation; he talked about undulating waves of air from musical instruments, or similar things that made a particular impression on the ear, as if the source of sound, the sound-source, were at close range. He spoke of generated tones and of pushing one of the buttons or starters that had been described; he spoke about the cycles of waltzes and the movements of a man, step by step, about the gradual movements of a man walking by, a man, or a figure in the shape of a man. He spoke in the style and manner that he, Fischer, had already described—or rather, in a way no one had ever yet described, no one, said Doctor Fischer, not a single person before me, since there are still attempts to keep these matters a secret, to keep secret the detailed information regarding the progress, as well as the order, and interests on the research on light, sound, and tone, or on research and studies in general, even in particularly favorable conditions, such as we have discovered here in Bad Orb, and are still discovering.

Fischer's bold address taught me to look at every event in a different light from that point on. When I resumed my observations, I noticed that several members of the Society of the Informal had disappeared from the circle of listeners. For example: Thiersch, Maß-mann, Malitz, Dietz, Ennmoser, Bertschi, Scherer, Beck, Lachner, Pechtl, and Zumbusch. Lemm was still among those present, as was Scheizhofer and Collunder, as Fischer's stirring words on the Society's continuous progress was followed by friendly applause in the casino ballroom. One of the attendants got up as he was applauding and disappeared. It was Dexberger: Dexberger, whose bloodlust and obsession with butchery immediately caught my attention; his blatant will to destroy and his unconditional desire for power and leadership, his feigned applause as his large black gloves barely seemed to touch. I observed this insidious deception as he disappeared under the posted beer advertisement, followed by his companions: men with faces like steel. Kobel and Förester were still applauding afterwards. In the next moment, Kobel had also disappeared.

I sat inconspicuously on the periphery of these events and was ready for anything. At which point it occurred to me that I was sitting on a hat. It wasn't my hat. This hat, I thought, could be the hat of the man sitting across from me, who was also sitting on a hat. However, it is not the hat of the man sitting across from me. Whose hat is it, I wondered, it's not mine, it's not my hat, but maybe it's the hat of the man sitting next to the man sitting across from me, or the hat of the man who just walked in and shouted: *Where's my hat!* It happened to be Dexberger, a somewhat confidence-inspiring vision. But before I continue to deal with Dexberger, I'll turn my attention—especially since this hat is of no concern to me—back to my reports and my observations.

And in this manner people come and go here, I wrote, coming in contact with things and situations, this is how differing opinions come together and clash here, in Bad Orb. With that I concluded my report on this gathering of the Informal. My assignment was fulfilled. Doctor Fischer lived, he bowed, and disappeared. I, too, got up and was satisfied that the tenth chapter had come to a good end; in any case an ending that wasn't all that bad, considering what it could've been under the circumstances outlined above.

11.
The Start of Chapter Eleven

At the beginning of chapter eleven, all of London was thrown into terror by a noise. Readers able to think back a few years will remember that I was in London at the time, in a hotel in Chelsea. I left the hotel and continued my dangerous life without any particular hurry. That sounds horrible, said the man sitting across from me as he folded his newspaper. I watched him in silence and noted that I could have, for example, filled the rest of this page with lists of every type of inconvenience that I met with in London and which were all, by the end, no longer inconveniences, but merely complaints about the superficial, external, general and boring inconveniences, the self-explanatory inconveniences everyone complains about in every place on earth.

As I walked out of the hotel in London, where I resided at the time, I heard a sound as if someone had broken a huge loaf of white bread in the air. Then I started to fall. I thought, apart from everything else and especially apart from myself: What's going on? Why are people looking at me? And then I saw in a shop window that I didn't look at all like I expected I would. I didn't recognize myself. I saw some blood running down a face, and it was possibly *my* face—it flowed out of me, onto the ground. It's blood, I said, it's blood flowing from a face and dripping onto the ground. It was not unpleasant to hear my voice, even though I believed it wasn't my voice. That was in London, September 5th. The man who sat across from me folded his newspaper. You could spare yourself plenty of anger if you'd just stop, remain seated, not write another word, and forget every word you wanted to write here, in this moment, he said, and departed. That was in '77, in a hotel in Chelsea.

In '78, one of my most important assignments was to observe a singer named Quint. I lived in Frankfurt and observed Quint from all sides, from below, looking up from the orchestra pit, from the balcony, from the box and from the gallery. As a matter of fact, I looked directly down at him through a hole in the ceiling, a secret window, but I didn't find anything that would have made this man suspicious. It's true he sang terribly; his pitches, especially his high pitches, were not his strength. Otherwise, there was nothing special to note. In the middle of '78, Quint left the opera, was in Vienna for a while and, after a long absence, showed up at the end of the year in the main train station, where I stood hidden behind a folded newspaper near a ticket machine.

I don't like describing this man's arrival, but I know I must. Quint approached me from the platform. What was most important was probably his head. His head was so much like a head that it was immediately thought of as a head and nothing more, if only because this head lifted itself up high in this moment and a body seemed to appear under it that looked so much like a body it could immediately be thought of as Quint's body, particularly indicative of many idiosyncrasies, other appearances, and characteristics. The face was hardly developed: it was virtually flat, it appeared eyeless, mouthless, hairless, as if it didn't have any orifices or expression. Everything about this man was short: his neck short, his head short, his legs and hair very short. The time in which I could describe everything was short, and the days were short, as were the nights with these numerous holes in the sky, the nights, the nights—what else? It was a shortness that was incomparable to any other shortness, at least not in this moment that I am talking about. And as he donned his hat in '78 on the edge of the platform, I noted: This hat swallows his head, his coat completely consumes him, his shoes eat up his feet, and his pants, together with his jacket, devour his body. The body of this man, who arrived from Vienna by express night train, was being slowly digested by his clothes. I noted all of it, I wrote everything down. If I'm honest about it, I must say that I was completely indifferent to everything. Because by the time this man had reached me at the ticket machine, there was nothing else left of him for me to describe.

There was another case in '79 that was more important than this case. I was living in Olm and was put in charge of finding a solution for the following matter. But the matter was so dangerous that I think it fit not to talk about it, even though talking about it would bring me pleasure. I also already knew how I could start, I could, of course, start something like *this*, which is only an example, an attempt, a possibility—but it would be a good start. So: *August '79* . . . No, that's not a good start. I could try it like *this: One day, in August '79* . . . I don't know, I'm not sure. Possibly like *this: One day, in the next chapter, sat* . . . No, worse than ever. But perhaps *this* could be the beginning: *In August '79, I looked in the mirror* . . . Yes . . . *I looked in the mirror* . . . That's it: *I looked in the mirror* . . . That could be a beginning.

12.
August '79

In August '79, I looked in the mirror and saw a peculiar, smile-like curl on my face. Perhaps it really was a smile. I sat at my desk and hoped to make an undaunted impression. Actually, I saw a rather fearless man sitting in the mirror who seemed to be ready for anything. Then for a while I didn't see anything else in the mirror. But then I did see something: as I lifted my hand, I saw a part of my raised hand that held a sharpened pencil. This image surely would have given me pleasure had I not been distracted by a ghostlike figure that suddenly sailed in. A woman dressed in black appeared in my office and began describing an event that pertained to her personally, a complicated event that reached back into to the past.

She acted so shy, so embarrassed, that I immediately began to think that she was unusually rude. She seems to me, I thought, to be a woman of great shamelessness, someone who will abuse my trust and kindnesses; a naked woman covered in clothes, covered from head to toe. An incredibly white body part only appeared here and there: her throat and hands, for example. I heard sentences that contained nothing, absolutely nothing from which one could infer her physical urges. But her message was so helpless and touching that I felt the salaciousness drain from me. An extraordinarily sleazy cleanliness caught my attention, an unrestrained restraint. Her gently lowered face and the handkerchief she used to cover a hiccupping sob; all of this was nothing other than the start of a massive debauchery.

I observed her dainty movements, how she opened her purse and took out her cigarette case. The act of opening it was alone so frivolous that my breathing faltered. The way she shut her purse—very gently, very carefully, almost without a sound—seemed to me to be the epitome of depravity. And finally, I found the innocent lighting of these endless cigarettes and the inhalation of smoke, which only reappeared after a great deal of time, to be nothing more than perfect deceit.

She spoke, and I was struck by her determination *not* to notice me, to not even seem aware of me. But I heard her speaking. She talked about something slashed open, about discreet, muffled shots, about faint pricks, tiny blows with a hammer—a very small hammer—or rather, blows with an expensive statue that she found in a display case. She said all of that gently, quite calmly. During this time it grew dark, and as I glanced in the mirror upon turning on the desk lamp, I saw a man who looked familiar—a man frozen in the act of listening.

Now I'm sitting here, telling you all of this and you're listening to me, said the woman dressed in black. It's lovely how you listen, Sir, you literally draw the words from my mouth; you find it nice, you find it interesting, don't you. You listen to me and enjoy it, you enjoy that you've found me to be guilty, that you got everything out of me in a single moment simply by listening, simply through your presence, by simply sitting, sitting without saying a word. You sit there, Sir, and I'll talk; I'll make use of words while you remain silent. And when I put a hole through your head with this pretty little revolver—because you want that—I'll make it more gentle than anything you've ever experienced. You're surprised you're hearing all of this, and of course you know that you have absolutely no chance of avoiding my words; you have no chance of escaping the consequences of the following words: Now I'll have the pleasure of shooting you, but naturally just a little, so that it doesn't draw more attention. Also, there won't be a bang. You'll continue to sit there as if nothing happened, not saying a word, and no one will see when I leave and you stay behind. You won't notice the blood at all as it flows over your face and drips on your carpet. You'll ask me to stay a little longer; you'll wish that I'd explain more about all of these things, these things you have no idea about, and you won't approve at all when you see me walk out into the snow; you'll follow my footprints, try to find me, discover me, and convict me, in the snow, won't you, Sir? You'll finally discover me in the snow, you'll see me lying there, covered by a thin layer of snow, blown over by the wind. You'll point at me, without a word, of course, and believe that you found me, and you'll find the opening in my head, the bullet hole in the back of my head. The blood will be frozen and my entire face will look like it's covered in powder, and you'll have seen nothing more beautiful in your entire life than blood in the snow, and through your presence alone, this story will lead to an interesting ending, in the snow covering my face like powder—won't it?

In the meantime I had forgotten how I looked, and because I hadn't looked in a mirror for quite some time, I forgot more and more. And when I finally did look in the mirror, I didn't know if it was *me* who sat at the desk and listened.

In August '79, in the dead of night, a woman appeared. I had never seen this woman before. She entered my office, approached me, lifted her hand and stuck her finger in my ear without a word, but then disappeared before the conclusion of this silent event. Her sweet perfume hung in the air for a while as I turned my attention to another issue. I got up to leave my office. I didn't know which direction I should head in, maybe left or right, presumably down the stairs, into an unknown place, where I knew with certainty that something new would be waiting for me. That, Ladies and Gentlemen, was it, what I wanted to share with you. Thank you for your attention.

Ror Wolf is an artist (surreal collages), an author of prose and poetry (much of which has been collected in a nine-volume series), and a writer of radio plays and "radio collages." Born in the East German city of Saalfeld, Wolf left the GDR for West Germany at the age of 31. His writing has earned him many awards, including Radio Play of the Year (2007), the Kassel Literature Prize for Grotesque Humor (2004), and the Literature Award of the Bavarian Academy of Fine Arts in 2003. Wolf's work has been translated into over 12 languages.

Jennifer Marquart studied German and translation at the University of Rochester. She has lived, continued her studies, and taught in Cologne and Berlin. *Two or Three Years Later: Forty-Nine Digressions* by Ror Wolf is her first book-length translation.

Open Letter—the University of Rochester's nonprofit, literary translation press—is one of only a handful of publishing houses dedicated to increasing access to world literature for English readers. Publishing ten titles in translation each year, Open Letter searches for works that are extraordinary and influential, works that we hope will become the classics of tomorrow.

Making world literature available in English is crucial to opening our cultural borders, and its availability plays a vital role in maintaining a healthy and vibrant book culture. Open Letter strives to cultivate an audience for these works by helping readers discover imaginative, stunning works of fiction and poetry, and by creating a constellation of international writing that is engaging, stimulating, and enduring.

Current and forthcoming titles from Open Letter include works from Argentina, Bulgaria, Denmark, France, Latvia, Netherlands, Poland, Russia, and many other countries.

www.openletterbooks.org